"No." Emily shook her head. "I'll never get involved with someone in a family business again…" She halted, aware of what she'd just said, but Alejandro just laughed at her discomfort.

"Good," he said, "because I don't do involved relationships." He was serious then. "Breakups don't have to be hard. People just make them so."

"I think it depends if you're the one doing the breaking up…"

"No," he cut in. "Why not just agree from the start it goes nowhere? Enjoy each other for however long and then walk away without regret."

Alejandro made it sound like an invitation, as if he was inviting himself on her adventure. They drove in silence but the words hung between them as she played them over and over, wondering if, by some chance, he was talking about them.

He made it sound so easy, so uncomplicated.

Could it be?

Heirs to the Romero Empire

A brand-new sizzling Spanish miniseries from
USA TODAY *bestselling author Carol Marinelli*

Siblings Sebastián, Alejandro and Carmen Romero
are heirs to a renowned sherry empire in Spain.
To the world, they have it all: charm, status and
wealth. But their parents' stormy marriage has
also left the siblings with a legacy of emotional
wariness, which has meant the empire always
came before love. Now, is that all about to
change?

Find out in Alejandro's story,
His Innocent for One Spanish Night

And look out for Sebastián's and Carmen's stories,
coming soon!

Carol Marinelli

HIS INNOCENT FOR ONE SPANISH NIGHT

ISBN-13: 978-1-335-73921-6

His Innocent for One Spanish Night

For questions and comments about the quality of this book, please contact us at CustomerService@Harlequin.com.

Harlequin Enterprises ULC
22 Adelaide St. West, 41st Floor
Toronto, Ontario M5H 4E3, Canada
www.Harlequin.com

Printed in U.S.A.

Recycling programs for this product may not exist in your area.

Carol Marinelli recently filled in a form asking for her job title. Thrilled to be able to put down her answer, she put "writer." Then it asked what Carol did for relaxation and she put down the truth—"writing." The third question asked for her hobbies. Well, not wanting to look obsessed, she crossed her fingers and answered "swimming"—but, given that the chlorine in the pool does terrible things to her highlights, I'm sure you can guess the real answer!

Books by Carol Marinelli

Harlequin Presents

Cinderellas of Convenience

The Greek's Cinderella Deal
Forbidden to the Powerful Greek

Scandalous Sicilian Cinderellas

The Sicilian's Defiant Maid
Innocent Until His Forbidden Touch

Those Notorious Romanos

Italy's Most Scandalous Virgin
The Italian's Forbidden Virgin

Visit the Author Profile page
at Harlequin.com for more titles.

For Anne and Tony.

Love always,

Carol xxxx

CHAPTER ONE

'I CAN'T JUST upend everything and move to southern Spain!' Emily Jacobs shook her head at the impossibility of it all. 'I have commitments here.'

'No,' Anna corrected, nodding towards her daughter Willow, who was running ahead, delighting in the crisp snow and a visit from her godmother. 'I'm the one who has commitments. As of three months ago, you have precisely none.'

'But I told Gordon I'd stay until the business was sold...' Emily started, and then paused, because it was in fact the other way around. Gordon had told *her* that she could stay in the bed and breakfast they had run together until it was sold...

He'd said it as if he were doing her a favour—as if he were making some magnanimous gesture, letting her stay on.

In truth, they hadn't run it together. The business had belonged to his mother, and when she'd recently died Gordon had rather brutally broken off their engagement...

Emily had quickly found out that she was considered as staff.

Live-in staff.

She'd had her own room in the large residence, respecting Gordon's religious beliefs and his wishes to wait until they were married to share a bed.

Emily hadn't told her best friend that part.

Surely people would laugh—ask why she'd stayed when he so clearly didn't want her...

Only she'd been too close to make sense of those things.

With no experience to compare, all Emily knew was that his kisses had held no promise. If anything, they'd tasted of reluctance.

His hands had never roamed.

Only once.

And even then he'd abruptly dropped contact and told her she was 'on the chubby side'.

So she'd lost weight, only he hadn't noticed.

So she'd put it back on, and he hadn't seemed to notice that either.

Always shy and uptight, she had felt the little confidence she had possessed evaporate, and she'd swung between blaming herself for his lack of passion and reassuring herself that it would change once they married.

Now, on a bright February afternoon, with the sky so blue it might well belong to summer, she was starting to see things more clearly—Gordon had never wanted a sexual relationship with her and had simply used her as a front to appease his mother.

He had never wanted her.

Not for a moment.

And that was the reason why, despite being in a relationship for five years, and engaged for three of them, at the age of twenty-six she was a virgin.

'Willow, wait!' Anna said, dashing ahead to catch

up with her energetic four-year-old, who was now running towards the frozen lake. 'Goodness…'

Emily laughed as her friend caught up with her child, but she didn't pick up her pace to catch up with them. It was nice to walk alone for a brief moment.

The time spent with her friend and daughter was actually refreshing.

Could she simply leave?

Take this rare chance and go?

An old university friend, Sophia, had called her just a couple of days ago with an offer. They'd kept loosely in touch via social media, but her call had come out of the blue.

'I'll need an answer soon,' Sophia had warned. 'I'm going on maternity leave and I want this sorted. Anyway, the brothers want a fresh perspective. They want to appeal more to tourists. Everyone in Jerez knows already how incredible it is… I showed Alejandro what you did with the website for that cottage where you work.'

Emily hadn't corrected Sophia and told her it was actually a bed and breakfast where she lived.

'He was impressed. And with the restaurant too…'

Since the break-up, Emily had been trying to get her website design business off the ground. Sophia's offer shot every ball out of the park. It was huge and utterly unexpected and, for the incredibly shy Emily, simply daunting.

This was not a simple job. Her potential clients wanted perfection and they were certainly willing to pay for it.

'Six weeks, with accommodation and transport,' Sophia had said. 'And there'll be a generous bonus if the website is up and running on time.'

The bonus was indeed generous—the whole package was.

Worryingly so!

Emily only had two clients. Her business was supposed to be building slowly—not exploding with offers such as this. She felt underqualified and far too inexperienced and had fought not to say as much.

'Think about it,' Sophia had said. 'I'll need an answer by Monday.'

With such a big decision to make, Emily had taken an extremely rare day and night off to spend time with Anna, her most trusted friend. They had grown up together in a tiny English village and were sometimes mistaken as sisters. Not so much in looks—Anna's hair was paler than Emily's dark blonde, while Emily was curvy, Anna was slender, and where Emily was timid, Anna was bold—but there was such a bond between them that at times it would be easy to assume they were sisters.

Anna and Willow were all the family that Emily had.

Was that why she'd been so accepting of the inadequacies in her and Gordon's relationship? Had she wanted a family so much that she'd chosen to settle for crumbs?

'Look at you!' Emily smiled at her goddaughter. She was wearing a coat and boots, a hat and gloves and huge ear muffs, due to some problems with her ears, but her teeth were chattering even as she pulled on her mum's hand to break free. 'You're freezing.'

'I don't care,' Willow said. 'I want to go and skate on the ice.'

'No!' her mother and her godmother said in unison.

'Those other children are...' Willow pouted as she was dragged reluctantly away. But she soon cheered up as they walked out of the park towards the village.

'She's too fearless...' Anna sighed.

'Like her mother!' Emily smiled. 'You used to go on the ice when we were little.'

'Yet you never did,' Anna said, turning her head. Emily could feel her eyes on her. 'You were always...'

'Chickening out?'

'I was going to say you were always sensible.'

'I wanted to go on it,' Emily admitted. 'I was just...'

'Scared?'

'Not so much of the ice cracking...' Emily sighed. 'I think I was scared of disappointing them.'

She thought of her mum and dad, they had been older than most of her friends' parents, and they had worried incessantly. Wrapping her up not in cotton wool, but in awful homemade cardigans, homemade scarves, homemade hats. Standing at the end of the drive wearing tense expressions if she was five minutes late home... While she'd been a little embarrassed at times, she'd felt so loved—but also so responsible for their happiness.

If ever there was a time to be brave and make changes Emily knew it was now, but despite being just out of a relationship and soon out of a home, she did have some commitments.

'There's the business sale...' Emily reminded Anna.

'Emily, you're not even going to get a share of the proceeds of the sale. You'll be left with nothing while Gordon will be off living his best life.'

Anna stopped talking then, clearly trying not to rub salt into her wounds.

Actually, there were no wounds.

She and Gordon's relationship had never been passionate enough for that.

'Tell him to take care of the sale of his own business,' Anna said. 'He's used you enough.'

Emily said nothing, just pressed her lips together so that her tense breath blew white out of her nostrils.

'Mummy, look!' a delighted Willow said as she ran back to them. 'Emily's a dragon.'

'Half-dragon,' Emily said, taking her goddaughter's hand on one side as Anna did the same on the other. 'Whole dragons breathe fire.'

'Are you really half-dragon?' Willow asked.

'I'm trying to be,' Emily said, and nodded, wishing she did have an inner dragon she could summon. A bit of fire to her spirit. Because as they tramped towards Anna's little home Emily knew that where Gordon was concerned she'd been more than a bit weak.

Where *everything* was concerned.

She should have resumed her studies in business and hospitality, but instead she'd taken the easier option and moved in with Gordon and his mother and worked in their family business.

It was nice to talk it through with Anna. Though Anna could be rather blunt at times, Emily appreciated it, for there was a decision to be made.

'So?' Anna broke into her thoughts. 'You met Sophia at university…?'

'Yes.' Anna nodded. 'She was in the Spanish group I went to.'

It had been a part of university she'd loved. A group that had paired up Spanish students with those learning the language.

'And you've stayed friends?'

'A bit...' Emily nodded. 'Well, we follow each other online. She saw my photography there, and the work I'd done for the B&B website, and the one for that restaurant chain...'

'Things are starting to take off for you.'

They were.

Her purchase of an expensive camera body had been far from impulsive, and had been the most money Emily had ever spent at once in her life. Gordon hadn't exactly been encouraging, and she'd felt dreadful spending the money left by her frugal parents on something so extravagant, but she knew if she was going to make a career out of website design then she needed the best equipment she could afford.

Slowly Emily had saved and added to her camera with various lenses and lighting equipment, and she had bought a tripod that, even though it had been second-hand, was fiercely expensive and, she was now realising, rather heavy.

'Six weeks seems like a long time to update a website...' Anna said.

'Not really... It's for some vast sherry bodega in Spain.'

'Vast?' Anna checked. 'I thought a bodega was a deli?'

'Not in Spain! The vineyards are out of town, but the bodega is where the barrels are stored and the sherry matured.' She'd been researching it since the second she'd hung up on Sophia. 'There are restaurants, *tabernas*, and the building itself is like a castle. It's more than a website makeover—they want a new one from scratch, as well as fresh images...'

'"They"?'

'It's a family business—though I think it's mainly run by two brothers. When they're there…' she added.

'Meaning…?'

'They sound like two spoiled playboys.'

Alejandro and Sebastián Romero, from everything she could glean, were as good-looking as they were depraved.

'It looks as if the whole of the Mediterranean is their playground.' Emily took a breath. 'I don't think I'm anywhere close to qualified to do it. This is a multimillion-dollar empire—multi*billion*, even…' Emily's eyes went wide at the prospect of such a huge client. 'They want a completely fresh take…for their business to be looked at through untainted eyes…'

'Virgin eyes?' Anna nudged her. 'Well, that's not you…'

It was, though.

And she felt very lonely with her secret.

Despite being so close to Anna, there were things Emily simply could not reveal, so she gave a tight shrug.

'I don't know anything about sherry,' she admitted. 'Well, I didn't. I honestly thought it was an old ladies' drink. Mum and Nanny always had one at Christmas…' Emily smiled fondly when she thought back to her childhood. 'It's a massive industry over there.' She gave a shaky laugh.

'In Jerez?' Anna checked, pronouncing it as it was spelt and then correcting herself, as Emily had done earlier. 'Sorry… *Hereth*!'

Emily laughed. 'I never thought sherry could be…' She looked over Willow's head and mouthed one word. *Sexy*.

It was Anna who laughed now, perhaps at the thought

of sherry being sexy. Or, more likely, at her rather up-tight friend who couldn't even say the word. And not just because they had a four-year-old walking between them.

'How?' Anna asked.

'I don't know…' Emily admitted.

She wanted to go to Jerez. She'd read about the rival bodegas, the dancing ponies and flamenco dancers, and it fascinated her.

It had been a lovely day, and all too soon Willow was in her pyjamas and pleading for Emily to read her a story.

'Of course,' Emily said, heaving herself up from the sofa.

'Emily's got a lot of phone calls to make,' Anna said, and then added. 'You *are* allowed to say no.'

'In this case, I don't want to.'

Willow chose the book—it was a motivational one, telling little girls to dream big.

'I could be a dragon when I grow up,' Willow said as she lay back on the pillow. 'And blow fire…'

'You'd be a wonderful dragon,' Emily agreed.

But then Willow shook her head at the idea. 'I'd melt the ice, though, and then I couldn't skate.'

'True.'

'I think I'll be a princess and an explorer,' Willow said, thinking out loud, 'and maybe I can be a unicorn at the weekends.'

'That sounds brilliant!' Emily smiled, and was about to offer another story, but an afternoon of playing in the snow meant Willow was already half asleep.

'You look pretty when you smile,' Willow said, 'though you don't smile very much.'

'I know…' Emily nodded. 'I think I was born with a serious face.'

That made Willow laugh, but then she had a question. 'What will you be, Em?'

'What do you mean, what will I be?'

'When you grow up?'

A Victorian spinster, Emily thought, though of course she didn't say that.

'I'm twenty-six,' Emily settled for saying. 'That's pretty grown up.'

'Not for unicorns.'

Having wished her goodnight, Emily gently closed the door. She could hear Anna, busy in the kitchen, but instead of heading straight down Emily sat on the stairs, grateful again for a moment of peace amongst friends.

Most of the photos on the walls by the stairs she had taken herself.

Willow's christening…her first birthday…

One tiny picture had the Jacobs and Douglas families together.

It had been taken at a fete in the next village, during the Christmas break of their final year at university… Anna's father had been the busy vicar, her mother the loyal vicar's wife.

Anna had told Emily that very day that she was pregnant and was terrified as to her parents' reaction.

Rightly so, as it had turned out.

Emily looked at her own father, so frail in a wheelchair, smiling for the camera without really knowing what was going on. Emily looked more carefully and could see the exhaustion in her mum's eyes. Just a month later she'd died.

"'Now is the winter of our discontent...'" Anna had said, given she'd been studying *Richard III* at the time.

Worse than a winter of discontent, though, Emily knew she had almost settled for a life of *almost* content.

There had been no contentment to be found in her lonely bed.

There was no contentment when you were in your twenties and being kissed by your fiancé as if you were some visiting great-aunt.

Emily didn't care that Gordon was undoubtedly gay. She just wished she'd known from the start, rather than waste five years wondering what was wrong with her.

Hell, they could have been honest friends, instead of faking a relationship.

You stayed because it suited you!

The thought she had been suppressing popped unwelcome into her head and Emily tensed as she faced it. Usually she'd stuff that thought right back down rather than admit to herself the truth—she hid from life. And always had.

As a child she'd been painfully shy, and having overprotective parents had felt like a blessing rather than a curse. She'd had the perfect excuse—that she couldn't take risks for fear of upsetting them. But, more honestly, she'd chosen not to take risks because they terrified her shy self.

It wasn't just in the big things that Emily held back. To this day she dressed conservatively and cut her own hair rather than sit in a salon chair and face scrutiny.

She checked her phone, her heart sinking when she saw it was Sophia, her rushed writing a mixture of Spanish and English.

Big NYC contract negociaciones. Los hermanos want the website changed. Permiso por maternidad from Monday, so need you there tomorrow. Puedes? Sophia

Tomorrow?

Emily re-read the message, her rusty Spanish telling her that Sophia was taking her maternity leave early, which meant there would be no one familiar to show her the ropes—and that was terrifying enough.

And Sophia's *'Puedes?'*—*'Can you?'*—was very direct.

She clearly wasn't going to plead—if Emily didn't want the work, then she'd have no trouble finding someone else.

Was she going to let another opportunity pass her by?

Emily wanted adventure and travel…

This was both.

And maybe, when the work was over, she might stay on in Spain for a little while longer and take care of another thing she'd long been neglecting.

Romance.

She wanted to find out how it felt to be kissed with passion.

As for sex?

She didn't know her own body, and she wanted to.

Yes, a holiday romance might just be on the agenda…

She sat for a few more moments and then made a call—only it wasn't to Sophia. Finally, taking a breath, she headed into the living room.

'I just called Gordon,' she said in a shaky voice. 'I've told him I'm moving overseas to take on a new job and I'll be leaving in the morning.'

'Yay!' Anna squealed, and jumped forward to embrace her, but Emily shook her hand to stop the contact, not quite ready to celebrate yet.

'He's very upset…' Actually he'd seemed more upset than he had been about the break-up! 'He said I should have given him more notice…'

'He gave *you* no notice,' Anna snorted.

'I'm going for it,' Emily said, her voice coming clearer now that her decision was made. 'I'll call Sophia now and tell her I'm taking the role.'

Emily did so, injecting enthusiasm into her voice to mask the terror she felt. 'I'll sort out the flights tonight…' She listened for a moment. 'Oh, that's fine. I'm hardly going to be there…'

They chatted for a few moments, and when Emily had concluded the call she filled Anna in.

'Sophia's hoping to meet me, but if not her husband will. Oh, and the apartment I was meant to be staying in has been booked by mistake—the flamenco festival is on—so I'm staying in the housekeeper's apartment.'

'With the housekeeper?' Anna screwed up her nose.

'I hope not!' Emily's head was spinning! 'It's all going too fast…'

'If you think about it, you'll never go.'

'True,' Emily admitted. 'Anna…' She looked up at her. 'I never wanted to go on the ice—it wasn't just because of my parents.'

'I know.' Anna smiled.

'And I have nothing to wear…'

The age-old problem was, in Emily's case, true. Her clothes consisted of stretch trousers and plain tops, all in muted greys and blacks. She wore the same all the time, as the trousers were good for crouching, as she had to for her photography. They were boring, practical.

'I actually have nothing to wear.'

'There are shops in Jerez! There are even hair salons,' Anna said.

Emily tensed as her friend teasingly touched a raw nerve. 'I've been looking it up while you read to Willow. It looks incredible, actually…'

It did.

Emily booked her flights, allowing for a couple of weeks' free time at the end. And when she should have been at home, packing her case and gathering together her equipment for tomorrow's flight, instead she looked at images of the stunning city that awaited her.

'I'm going to say yes to everything,' Emily vowed.

'And that starts with being able to say no,' Anna said. 'Just be yourself, Emily. It doesn't matter whether or not they like you, so long as they love your work.'

Anna was so bold, and Emily desperately wanted to be, so she nodded. 'I'm just…' She wanted to try new things, make up for the lost years. 'I'm just going to go for it!'

CHAPTER TWO

ALEJANDRO ROMERO WOULD prefer this conversation, this day, this week, to be over.

Given it was late on a Sunday evening, it soon would be.

Not that Mariana would accept the end.

'You tell me our relationship is over in a *cellar*?' she shouted.

'I told you we were finished in December,' he responded calmly. 'It's February now.'

As well as that, it was hardly a cellar.

The Romero bodega was a short walk from the gorgeous Plaza de Santiago, with its churches and cafés and gorgeous shops and fountain. They stood under spectacular wooden arches in what had once been a church. The room was beautifully lit, with the moon streaming through a small stained-glass window. The location was coveted, its contents were worth millions, the archways spectacular, the artwork stunning—but, when Mariana regaled people with the tale she would, of course, say that Alejandro Romero had dumped her in a cellar.

For good.

Not that Mariana was listening.

'Alejandro, si significo algo para ti, por favor no

hagas esto.'—'Alejandro, if I mean anything to you, then please don't do this now.'

'Now?' Alejandro demanded. 'Mariana, what do you mean "now"? I told you that we were through before Christmas…'

'But then we found out about your father.' She grabbed his jacket. 'At least wait until—'

'When?' he cut in. 'It will never be a good time for our families.'

'Your father is dying!' she wailed, but he stood there unmoved.

Alejandro loathed drama. Yes, drama—because it wasn't, nor had it ever been, a romance, and it was nothing to do with love.

'You are an emotional wasteland, Alejandro.'

He shrugged.

'Listen to me… Let him go to his grave thinking our bodegas will merge.'

'I would expect my father has another year,' Alejandro said. 'If he has surgery, it could give him even more than that. And I will tell you now, I don't intend to stay celibate that long.'

'You're such a bastard, Alejandro. It's always about sex with you.'

'Yes,' he said. 'And don't tell me you haven't benefited from our arrangement. I don't want marriage, Mariana. I don't want to play these family games any longer.' He removed her hand from his arm. 'Tell your family, and tell your friends, that we are over—because if you don't, I shall. I don't love you, Mariana.' He was blunt, but it was the truth, and nothing he hadn't said before. 'And you don't love me.'

'Which is exactly why we are perfect together.'

She ran a hand along his tense jaw and tried to push his thick black hair back from his eyes, but Alejandro removed her hand.

'You don't believe in love and I don't need it…'

She had an answer for everything, and, in many ways she was right. Alejandro did not believe in love. If it did exist, then he didn't want it. He'd seen what it had done to his father.

'Don't do this now,' she warned. 'You cannot do this to your father. It would devastate him.'

'Mariana, we're over.'

'Until the next woman you date gets stars in her eyes and doesn't know how to handle you. Until she starts wanting more. Then you'll realise how good we had it.'

She reached for his groin and he pushed her hand away. 'Go home,' he told her, peeling her off him as she tried to kiss him, her red lips too much for his dark mind tonight.

She smeared his face with her lipstick and then laughed as he pulled his head back.

'Go home,' he said again.

'I'll see you when you're lonely,' she sneered, before flouncing off. 'After the summer, maybe?'

'We're done.'

He stood in the semi-darkness, relieved that they were over but doubting himself as to the timing.

Alejandro knew he was—as Mariana had accused him of being—an emotional wasteland. He found life far easier to negotiate without emotions.

He worked hard and he partied harder.

And, while he did both vigorously, it was all with a certain air of dispassion that infuriated his lovers but impressed his associates and his peers.

I don't care. That was the message behind his dark brown eyes and his indifferent shrugs.

No one was allowed to get too close, and he rarely revealed his innermost thoughts.

His father though, was the opposite.

The news would indeed upset him.

Yet Mariana had spoken as if it might devastate him.

José Romero seemed rather more willing to lie down and die than fight at the moment, and Alejandro certainly didn't want to add to his malaise.

Alejandro could hear laughter and conversation wafting over from the fine dining restaurant in the main courtyard. He'd have to walk through it to get to his gated residence. But instead of heading for home he made his way to the front of the bodega and entered the rather exclusive Taberna Romero.

'Hola!' A waitress smiled a welcome, and so did a few customers, but Alejandro just nodded—he was really not in the mood for polite conversation tonight.

The place was often packed, but it was especially so this Sunday night, when there were flamenco performers on stage. Glancing at the set list, he realised it was Eva performing.

The trouble with being at home, Alejandro thought as he slid into a seat in the booth reserved for the Romeros, was that there were rather too many exes.

Eva had been his first lover.

And that had been a *very* long time ago.

He heard the stamp of boots on the wooden stage and the tempo shifting as the lights dimmed further, but he barely looked up. Too many reminders tonight.

He could recall sitting backstage in Barcelona or Madrid as his mother performed—she'd long since outgrown smaller venues by then. He recalled, too, the accusations by his father when she came home…and then his dreadful depression when she no longer did.

His brother Sebastián and his sister Carmen loathed their mother with a passion, yet Alejandro could see his mother's side too.

If his father could just have been more accepting and understood her talent, her art…

And flamenco *was* an art.

He just couldn't bring himself to watch, so instead of looking at the stage he glanced around the *taberna*. It was mainly filled with locals, all looking forward to Eva performing, and there were several of her dance students in attendance.

And then he saw a woman who was definitely *not* a local.

It wasn't just her blonde hair that made her stand out, but the way she sat nervously, twiddling her hair, sipping wine, looking so out of place and just plain awkward. Her top was too tight, her hair had either been whipped by the wind or cut with a hand whisk, and he watched as she picked up a shot glass of *puré de guisantes* and sniffed it, as if trying to work out what it was.

She didn't quite hold her nose, but she knocked it back in one and then pulled such a face that he found he held his breath. Finally she gulped it down with a large sip of wine.

And then shivered.

Like a little dog shaking itself off.

And as her breasts moved her hair did too, and brought a rare smile to his features.

Next she tried to chase an olive with a fork, rather than pick it up with her fingers.

He saw the camera on the table beside her and realised that this was perhaps Emily Jacobs, the English woman who was here to do the photography and design for the new website.

He should go over and introduce himself, but he could not be bothered to make polite conversation tonight. Anyway, she looked miserable. She had now given up chasing reluctant olives, and looked as if she was about to leave just as the main act came on!

God, maybe he should have listened to Sebastián and used someone tried and trusted rather than go for the fresh slant recommended by Sophia...

But then she looked up.

Not at him.

She looked up to the stage.

He knew from the stamping, from the shouts of approval and from the dimming lights, that Eva was about to perform, and that she would be standing poised on the now-dark stage, but still he did not turn around.

Alejandro watched Ms Jacobs instead.

And he knew then that his much opposed decision to bring in an outsider had been the right one.

He watched as her expression shifted from weary to alert...how she sat up straighter in the hard wooden seat as the stage lights lifted and she witnessed for the first time true flamenco.

Her food was forgotten, her eyes wide and fixed on the dancer, her mouth open just a little. Her white shirt strained a little across the bust, and yet somehow her very plain outfit was subtly beautiful.

She was beautiful.

Gone was the slouch and the attempt to fade into the surroundings.

There was now an expression of rapture on her face that perhaps should have him turning to the stage and watching the performance.

Alejandro simply preferred watching her...

It was as close to magic as Emily had ever seen.

Her rushed journey to Jerez had proved incredibly long. There had been no Sophia nor her husband to greet her at Jerez Airport—just a man holding a sign bearing her name, who'd offered Sophia's apologies and given her an envelope.

The note had said that Sophia would catch up with her for breakfast tomorrow, but tonight she'd suggested Emily dine at the *taberna* and get a feel for the place. Also that Eva was performing.

Emily had had no idea what that meant.

She would by far have preferred to sit alone in the thankfully vacant housekeeper's apartment that she'd been shown to rather than venture out, but it would be for work.

More than that.

She'd been hungry.

As well as that, this was her new career—her long-awaited adventure. And so, before she'd changed her mind, she'd headed down to the *taberna*.

She'd asked for a table for one and then, a little overwhelmed by the menu, at the waitress's suggestion had ordered a selection of tapas.

A rather delicate selection had arrived, which hadn't quite matched her ravenous appetite.

There'd been a few guys quietly strumming guitars

on stage, and the atmosphere had been friendly, but sitting alone eating dishes best shared she'd felt awkward and exposed.

Emily had just given up on the tapas and had been reaching for her camera, ready to leave...when the magic had started to happen.

The stage had gone dark and Emily had looked up as the noisy venue had hushed. Either her eyes had become accustomed to it, or it was a trick of the lighting, but she could just make out the silhouette of a woman, centre stage, one arm raised above her head. And as the lights lifted Emily saw the woman's other arm moving slowly, making gentle waves, as if with a life of its own.

This must be Eva, she quickly realised. The performer Sophia had suggested she come to the *taberna* to watch.

Eva was stunning.

Her black curls were pinned up, her make-up dramatic and her neck taut and slender. Her dress was the same vibrant yellow as rape fields in summer, the fabric not unlike flowers moving in the wind. Emily sat high on her seat to get a better look, utterly transfixed as Eva commenced a slow, sensual dance.

It was spellbinding.

Eva clapped, making a sharp noise with the strike of her hand, and then she beat out the tempo with her black shoes and the men matched it with their music.

Eva smiled and growled and bared her teeth, portraying every emotion as she moved, demanding that the musicians match her changing moods.

The dancing pushed them on.

It was incredible.

There was nothing Emily could do but watch as Eva's elegant body and strong gestures held the entire room.

The noise of her shoes, the thunder of the men's boots and the increasing tempo from the guitars, as well as the percussion instruments two of the men held between their thighs, seemed to be building towards a crescendo.

Yet, they continued on.

Eva's claps were like whips being cracked, precise and demanding, and then suddenly more muted.

The men clapped too, now, as if urging her to new limits, attempting to exhaust her. And yet she refused to relent, striking the stage so fast that Emily felt as if she were caught in a sudden hailstorm, struck by a power she could never hope to override.

How, Emily begged herself, had she not known this world existed?

She wanted to move, to get up and dance as some of the customers were doing. She wanted to shout out and cheer like the other patrons. She could feel herself smiling, even taking a sip of her wine and raising her glass in appreciation at one point.

It was hypnotic, incredible… But then, as a woman stood up from a table to get closer to the stage, Emily briefly turned, and although the *taberna* continued to heave with music and dance, and the music poured forth, for Emily it all seemed to pause.

He stopped her with his gaze.

He wore a dark suit.

Some other patrons did too, but they were end-of-work-day suits, with jackets off, shirtsleeves rolled up.

Casual.

This man was far from that.

His tie was loosened, his jaw unshaven, and yet he was utterly immaculate.

And he was bold with his dark eyes.

Emily had never been looked at like that before.

Had never looked back at another person with such intensity in her entire life.

It truly felt as if it would be entirely appropriate for him to walk over to her right this moment, or for him to beckon her to him.

She sat there on the hard wooden chair, feeling the thunder of boots reverberating from the stage, and the patrons, but they were tiny jolts compared to the sheer effect of this man.

The music returned—it had never left—and her senses also returned, as if a long drink was being poured, filling her from her thighs upwards, low, low in her stomach—which she held in. Not just because she all too often held it in—he couldn't see that anyway—simply because it was clenched and guarded against the heat of his stare. And still he filled her senses as the music played on. She could feel her breasts grow heavy in her bra, feel her throat too tense even to swallow.

And as for her mouth…

It felt too big for her face…her lips out of position. And without a word being spoken, with barely a moment between them, she was more turned on than she had ever been in her life.

It was the music, she told herself, dragging her eyes from his face. Surely it was the music or the effects from the wine?

Yet the carafe on her table was still almost full, she realised at a glance, trying to fathom what was taking place.

It was his beauty, she told herself as she reached for that final olive, stabbing it with a little fork and missing.

Damn.

She dipped some bread in oil and tried to pretend she could not feel a pulse where she'd thought none existed.

It startled her—to be in public and for the first time turned on. So much so that she wanted to dash to the loo…to escape. To flee from the rush of unfamiliar sensations and the intensity of a man she hadn't even met.

Emily simply reverted to type…

And fled.

Mujeres, it said on the door. There was a little picture of a woman in a flamenco dress, and Emily was grateful for it, because second language skills were not at the forefront of her mind at the moment.

It was empty—thank goodness.

Of course they were all still watching Eva perform.

She could hear the shouts and the music. It was the music that was affecting her so strongly, Emily told herself as she stood in the very pretty ladies' room.

There were huge mirrors on the walls with velvet chairs placed in front of them, as if it were some kind of dressing room. Emily stood there for a moment, taking in not so much the surroundings but her own reflection.

She wore the same black trousers and thin shirt that she'd left the apartment in.

That she'd left England in, come to that.

The same black court shoes…

Her hair was tangled and tied up, and her face, as always, was completely devoid of make-up.

Yet she was flushed.

Her lips were rosy, as if she'd been chewing them.

Her nipples were showing through her shirt.

And as she sat on a seat she noticed her dilated pupils and moist eyes, and felt as if something had been unleashed.

It has to be the music, she told herself.

Of course it was.

She kept trying to replay that second when everything had somehow shifted.

When the lights had dimmed?

Or was it when the clapping had started?

The stamping of boots, perhaps?

When she'd locked eyes with him?

The door opened and, ridiculously, she almost expected it to be the man whose eyes she'd locked with. Quickly she told herself she wasn't thinking straight—she was surely sleep-deprived, jet-lagged…

Sex-starved.

She laughed out loud at that.

Oddly, it didn't seem to be out of place, because the young woman who now came in laughed also.

'*Ella es brillante, ¿no?*'—'*She's brilliant, isn't she?*' the lady said, taking a seat beside Emily and rearranging her rather spectacular bust.

'*Sí,*' Emily agreed, grateful that she understood what had been said, but not quite brave enough to respond in Spanish. 'I've never seen anything like it…' Her voice trailed off, but it didn't matter.

'She is the best.' The woman looked down at her lovely bust and, happy with her cleavage, took some lipstick from her purse. 'I go to her workshop.'

'Do you?'

'We come here for practice some days…' She caught Emily's eyes in the mirror. 'Are you English?'

Emily nodded, feeling incredibly drab beside this gorgeous, confident woman.

'I'm Stella.'

'Emily.'

'And are you here for a holiday?'

'For work,' Emily said, and yet it felt as if she was lying.

It felt as if she was here on an adventure.

An adventure of her own.

But then common sense returned.

'Damn!' she said suddenly, and saw the woman start. 'Sorry. I left my camera on the table.'

'No problem.'

She felt a little more composed as she walked out. Eva had stopped performing, or was taking a break, because the music was softer now and the lights had gone back on.

And her seat was taken.

The tapas and wine had been cleared away and at her table for one now sat a carefree group of four. There was no handbag—and, worse, there was no camera.

There was a moment of panic—she'd been careless enough to lose her possessions on her first night in Spain—but then she felt an odd calm…a quiet certainty that *he* wouldn't have allowed that to happen…and she turned her head to the mysterious stranger.

There were her things. On the table where he sat.

She felt again that curious calm as, with a slight gesture of his head, he beckoned her over.

And, as easily as that, Emily went.

CHAPTER THREE

'EMILY...' HE WAS POLITE, and thankfully he missed how startled she was that he knew her name because he moved to stand as she joined him. 'Sophia said that you were arriving today.'

It dawned on her then that he must be one of the brothers as he gestured for her to take a seat at his table.

No hard chair for a Romero, she thought as she took her place in a red velvet booth. And somehow, she managed to play it not cool—that would have been impossible with blood so hot it bubbled through her veins like lava—but at least she managed to appear outwardly poised.

'I'm Alejandro,' he said.

'The middle one?' she checked, trying to remember the little she knew of the Romero siblings.

'The reasonable one.'

'Good to know.'

'At least in comparison to the other two.'

She smiled. 'Sebastián and Carmen?'

'*Sí.*' he nodded. 'Would you like a drink?'

'I've had one,' Emily said. 'Or two...' She put her hands up to her cheeks, as if the wine was to blame for the flush to her face and neck.

He gestured to her camera and bag. 'The waitress brought your things over—she hadn't realised you were staff.'

'I didn't tell her…' Her hands reached for her beloved camera. 'For a second I thought I'd lost this.'

'No.' He shook his head. 'That wouldn't happen in here. Although it's a nice camera.'

'It's a bit…' She hesitated. 'Well, it felt a bit extravagant at the time.'

'But it's for your work.'

'Yes, but when I bought this it was really no more than a hobby.' She rolled her eyes. 'An expensive one. Almost all my baggage allowance was taken up with photographic equipment…'

Alejandro frowned just a little and it dawned on Emily that the Romeros, with their yachts and private jets, had probably never heard of a pesky little thing like baggage allowance.

'Well, you can always use this table if you need to be here to get photos of the stage or whatever.'

'Thank you.'

He was polite…almost formal. It was as if that odd moment when they'd stared at the other, when they'd locked gazes, hadn't happened. And really nothing *had* happened—just a look.

A look during which presumably he'd guessed the pale woman with a camera was his new employee.

It was her own mind that had gone wild.

He spoke with a rich Spanish accent. And, although perhaps it was the brighter lights as the stage was re-arranged, his features demanded scrutiny. His eyes, framed perfectly with dark arched brows, were every shade of brown and vividly revealed, because the whites of his eyes were the clearest she had ever seen. His mouth was pale and his lips were full, and she saw a smear of red lipstick on one side of his mouth...

Why did that last detail sting?

It was no business of hers who he'd been kissing—and anyway, even if he wasn't her boss, Alejandro Romero was completely out of her league. She was only sitting with him because she was staff.

He sat back a little, holding his glass loosely with long fingers as he made polite conversation. 'How was your trip here?'

She thought back to a few hours ago, and it felt like light years away. 'It was fine...well, a bit rushed.'

He just looked at her.

'There was a long wait in Madrid for my flight to Jerez...'

'There are a lot more direct flights from Seville.'

'Really?'

'It's an easier route. I'm surprised Sophia didn't arrange that.'

'I booked my own flights.'

'That's right—I know she's been unwell. Was she able to meet you?'

'No.'

'So you haven't been shown around?'

'Not yet,' Emily said, as if it didn't matter—as if she hadn't felt terrified and alone as she'd sat in the apartment.

And now here she sat in a *taberna*, face to face with the most stunning man.

Both had been overwhelming—though the latter was nicely so.

'So where are you staying?' he asked. 'In Plaza de Santiago?'

'No, I'm staying here…on the property,' Emily told him. 'Apparently the usual accommodation is unavailable, so I'm in the housekeeper's apartment.'

'We're neighbours, then…'

'Neighbours?'

'The residence here is mine.'

'Oh…'

Gosh, she'd glimpsed the beautiful building behind huge arched iron gates, never for a second thinking it might be somebody's home.

'Usually the staff stay in one of our residences in the *plaza*,' Alejandro said, and then he gestured to the stage. 'But the flamenco festival is about to commence, and your accommodation must have been booked out by mistake.'

'So there isn't usually live entertainment?' Emily asked. 'This is just for the festival?'

'Oh, no, there's always live entertainment,' he said. 'But it's rare that Eva performs.'

'She's incredible.'

'Indeed… There's generally a few performances in the afternoons, but with the festival coming up there will be a lot more.' He looked at her then. 'At night, the list is more informal. Spontaneous.' He looked towards the stage. 'It looks as if some of Eva's students are about to perform.'

'I didn't realise just how big flamenco was here,' Emily admitted. 'I mean, I thought it was…' Her voice trailed off; she was not sure he would appreciate how little she knew.

'Thought what?' he prompted.

'That it was something just put on for the tourists.'

'Oh, no.' He seemed to take no offence at her naivety. Clearly he had heard it many times before. 'They love the traditions here,' he explained. 'There are a lot of *peñas*…'

'Peñas?' Emily checked.

'It's a local term. Kind of…' he sought a translation for her '…a flamenco club where *aficionados* go.'

'Aficionados?' she repeated, and then worked out what he meant without explanation. 'Enthusiasts?'

He nodded.

'And are you one?'

'Not particularly,' he said.

He looked up as a waitress came over to top up his glass and shook his head. Emily had the feeling he was about to go, but then he looked at her.

'Have you tasted our sherry?'

'No,' she admitted. 'I did try to get hold of some, but I live in a small village and…'

'It's fine.' He spoke in rapid Spanish to the waitress and soon a bottle was brought over, and also a cheese board.

But it was the bottle that held her gaze.

She'd seen it online, of course, but the photos hadn't captured its beauty.

Yes, beauty.

Its glass was black and the cork was sealed with an amber resin that trickled down the side of the neck like melted candle wax.

It was a work of art in itself—so much so that she picked it up and read the label.

The words *Bodega Romero* were branded into the glass, and even the label itself was stunning.

At first glance it looked like a flower—an orange poppy, perhaps, with a dark centre—but on closer inspection she saw it was a photo of a flamenco dancer. The orange was the ruffles of her dress, the black centre her slick black hair in a bun...

'It's gorgeous,' she said, and then put the bottle down, watching his long fingers skilfully deal with the seal and the cork. She was nervous, but nicely so.

'Oloroso,' he said. 'It is probably the sherry you are more used to.'

'I'm not a big sherry drinker. I...' She hesitated, deciding it would be rude to say that she couldn't stand the stuff. 'Well, I'm not really a drinker.'

'It's fine,' he said again. 'Did you like the tapas?'

'Yes,' Emily said politely. 'They were delicious.'

'All of them?'

She felt her lips pinch on a smile at the doubt in his voice and realised he'd possibly seen her before she'd seen him.

'Not the pea puree in a shot glass...' She pulled a face. 'I'm sure they were beautifully prepared,' she added hurriedly. 'I just don't like peas...especially when they've been liquefied.'

'So why did you drink it?' he asked as he dealt with the bottle's seal.

'It's rude not to clear your plate.'

'The chef's not that sensitive.' He smiled a lazy smile and his teeth were as dazzling as the whites of his eyes.

God, he was gorgeous—and it wasn't just that he was easily the best-looking man she'd ever seen. Despite the sheer thrill of him, she felt a rare but certain sense of ease in his presence.

His movements were smooth as he poured the drink and conversation flowed just as easily.

'Did you see the little silver spoon on your plate?'

'Yes.'

'It's there so that you can taste a little, then decide.'

'I'll remember that in the future.'

'Good.'

She wanted to taste just a little, Emily thought as she looked at that lipstick-smeared mouth and wondered what it might be like to be kissed by him.

It was a brief thought.

A pointless one.

He was completely out of her league and that wasn't being self-effacing—Emily was simply being real. This was a tasting—a chance to test the product—nothing else.

It was just this tiny part of her mind that was raising objections… Saying this was something else.

Their eyes locked again as he raised his glass. *'Salude!'* he said.

'Cheers.' Emily smiled and, knowing he was watching her as she took her first sip of Romero sherry, felt terribly aware of her own mouth. In the oddest way, she actually wondered if the glass might miss her lips.

He must think her a nervous wreck, Emily was sure, because it took her two attempts to get the glass there, interspersed with nervous giggles.

Alejandro did not think her a nervous wreck. Just nervous, shy, and—unlike the sherry—very sweet.

He watched her take a sip, and her blue eyes closed as she held it in her mouth. Alejandro, who spent a lot of his life introducing sherry in tastings, found himself turned on by what should be just the usual.

She swallowed, and then opened her eyes, and out bobbed the tip of her pink tongue.

'Wow!' she said, and then began to take another taste, but halted herself as the aftertaste hit. 'Oh…' She smiled at him. 'Perhaps I do like sherry after all.'

'Or you're just being polite?'

'It's gorgeous,' she said. 'Though I have no idea about wines and such, so please don't ask me to describe its taste on the website.'

'Don't worry—that part's already written. This is a full-bodied sherry.'

Why did everything sound mildly inappropriate tonight? He found that he was fighting not to glance down to her rather full-bodied breasts.

Instead, he looked at what she was holding in her hands—the amber resin from the seal.

'You get to keep that.'

Emily looked up.

'It's tradition,' he said.

'Oh…' She looked at the beautiful amber resin she held between her fingers and could see the trapped wing of a butterfly within. It was a little like the way she felt…

The way she'd always felt.

Trapped by her own shyness.

Simply unable to fly.

'Now, cheese,' he said. 'Assuming you like cheese?'

'I do,' she agreed and, slipping the seal into her bag, she watched as he sliced slivers of cheese and gestured for her to take up a fork.

She hesitated. 'Actually, I don't like goats' cheese…'

'Okay.' He didn't even look up from the cheese he was slicing.

He did not know just how momentous a thing it was for Emily to state her preference.

'What about ewes' milk?'

'I don't know,' she admitted. 'It sounds dreadful, but…'

'It's soft…sweeter…'

Oh, 'the usual' was proving so much more difficult tonight.

She was telling him she was, in fact, starving, and that the tapas hadn't really sufficed.

'I didn't have time for breakfast, and there was nothing much left on the trolley.'

'The trolley?'

'On my flight,' she said, smearing creamy cheese over a delicate cracker. 'By the time they got to me all the sandwiches had gone.'

'Oh.'

It wasn't a problem he'd come across on the Romero private jet, or when he travelled first class, but the roll of her eyes as she told him her tale made him smile.

'Your business is new?' he asked.

'Yes. I've always been into photography, and when I was studying at university, there was a "How to develop a website" module. But…' She glanced up, aware she wasn't being very coherent. 'I didn't finish my degree.'

He nodded.

'Just so you know…'

'I didn't go through your CV, Emily. Sophia recommended you. We want the new website to be fresh and different…to better bring our product to the world,' Alejandro said. 'I suggested we get an outsider in and Sebastián agreed. Sophia showed us your work. I saw how you managed to make that dump of a cottage look quaint.'

Emily bristled at the put-down and wondered what to say—if anything. 'That was my home,' she said.

'Was?' he checked, not appearing even remotely embarrassed.

Possibly he didn't know that the word 'dump' was so offensive? she decided, giving him the benefit of the doubt.

'Yes.' She gave him a tight smile, wishing his question wasn't so pertinent.

This morning she'd left her home of five years, and she'd done so with barely a backward glance. Oh, she'd have to return and properly collect her things, but shouldn't it at least have hurt a little more?

For the first time the conversation stalled and, glancing around, she saw that the *taberna* was starting to empty.

A couple of the waiters were looking over at them.

Some of the patrons too.

Perhaps he noticed the same. 'I'm going to head off,' Alejandro said.

'And me,' Emily responded without thinking, and in rusty Spanish she asked the waitress for the bill for her tapas and wine.

'It's taken care of,' Alejandro told her. 'Dine here whenever you please. The staff will know who you are now. If there's someone new on, just let them know you work here.'

'Thank you.'

It was only as she stood that she felt a little awkward, realising they would be walking out together.

She put her camera over her shoulder and picked up her bag. And it really was awkward, because everyone seemed to want to farewell him as he walked out. As he stopped to talk to a couple, Emily felt it better that she leave him to it rather than stand there.

She left the *taberna* and made her way to the courtyard. She'd been too nervous to really notice it on her way to the *taberna*, but now, with most of the diners gone, she saw its beauty. To one side there were the cellars, but the courtyard itself was entrancing. Trees were delicately lit with fairy lights and laden with ripe oranges, their fragrance sweet as she passed. There was a rustic, elegant beauty to the place, and the lightly sanded ground softened her footsteps as she approached the arched gates—only to find them locked.

'Damn,' she muttered, wondering if she should go back and ask one of the bar staff for assistance, and feeling stupid for getting locked out on her first night.

'You have to go around to the back and sign in with Security after midnight.'

Alejandro had almost caught her up and called to her from across the courtyard.

'I see.'

'Unless,' he added, 'you're me.'

'Fine,' she said, and clipped off in shoes that were starting to hurt.

'Emily, wait.'

Her awkwardness seemed to mildly amuse him.

'I was teasing. I'm not going to make you walk around.'

He pressed in a code and the gate clicked open.

He proceeded to tell her the numbers as they headed through what must be his private grounds.

'I won't remember them,' Emily said, although she was grateful for the reprieve from walking further tonight.

'Why would you forget?'

'Because I'm dreadful with numbers.'

'But there are only four of them!'

He was taller than she'd realised. It felt a little like walking beside the headmaster as he asked her to repeat the code he'd just told her.

'I've already forgotten,' Emily admitted.

'Seriously?'

'I honestly have.'

They were climbing some steps, beautiful mosaic steps that led to more gorgeous arched gates, where they would part company.

He smelt incredible. His cologne was the sort that might make you close your eyes if you inhaled it in the perfume section of a department store. You'd start sniffing, trying to follow the delectable scent, just so you could douse your wrists in luxury for a while. It was the sort where you might have to turn to a complete stranger and ask what on earth they were wearing, because it was surely the most perfect scent in the world.

It was musky, but not heavy.

Citrussy, yet not any kind of citrus she knew.

And so fresh it served as a reminder that she'd been up since five, and on trains and planes, and...

Not so fresh.

How, at five minutes after midnight, did he look as if he were about to head for the office rather than bed?

Apart from the fading smear of lipstick and the heavy growth on his chin…

God, he was a cross between a bandit and the cleanest man she had ever seen.

And just so sexy.

And it was fun—just that—to talk to him, to stand and make idle, silly talk on this, her first night of new adventure. Safe in the knowledge that someone as completely divine as he, was surely not wanting anything of her.

Now she must go.

She would pull the massive key from her tiny bag and take her sore and no doubt swollen feet to bed for the night.

Except he was so nice to speak to…

And he seemed in no rush to go…

'Just use this entrance in future.'

'Okay.' She nodded. 'Thank you.'

'Can you remember the code now?'

'I've had a couple of sherries,' Emily said, but chose not to add that it wasn't the fortified wine making her feel a little dizzy.

She'd never known attraction before—at least nothing so intense. And she was so down on herself that it didn't enter her head that the feeling might be mutual.

'Come on—try and remember.'

'Four…?' She grimaced as she guessed.

'There's no four.' He gave her a look, a very deep and serious look that made her think, were he a doctor, she'd be terrified of his verdict. But in the periphery of her vision she could see his lips tilt slightly in a smile. And they weren't so pale now…they were a dark and very beautiful pink.

'*Think,*' those gorgeous lips said.

'Five?'

'Jesus!' He laughed. 'You really have no short-term memory.'

'Not when—' She stopped, deciding it would be foolish, at best, to tell him her lack of focus was entirely due to the scent in her nostrils and the absolute concentration it was taking to keep her hands at her sides, rather than...

Rather than what?

She didn't even want to examine that question—not with him so close.

It was a question to ponder later—only he still seemed in no rush to go, and he lounged against the iron gates and carried on talking.

'If you want to take flamenco lessons,' Alejandro said, 'Eva would be a good teacher for you.'

'Lessons?' Emily let out a nervous laugh. 'Gosh, no.'

It had never entered her head. Only Alejandro didn't join in with her smile or her burst of laughter.

It was, she realised, an actual suggestion.

He had no idea what a klutz she was.

'I don't think so.'

'You might like it. And as well as that...'

Alejandro paused. He had been about to say that he would love to see her practising, for Eva brought her pupils over to the courtyard or the *taberna* some evenings...

How he would love to see her ripe body move...

He held back.

This was an odd situation for Alejandro. Not so much the walking up the steps with a beautiful woman he'd met at the *taberna*. More that she would be turning left and he would be turning right, going through the gates to his own residence.

'As well as that…?' Emily checked.

Her blue eyes met his, yet he could not read her, and Alejandro was most unused to that. There was an energy between them—so much so that when he'd seen the staff and patrons looking their way he'd rather abruptly ended the night.

At least, he'd ended it for public consumption.

But now they were alone, and she was unreadable, only a little bold, and there was a certain reticence to her as if she did not know how to conclude the night.

Usually it would be with a kiss.

Usually, with an attraction so palpable, they would be tearing at each other's clothes by now.

But, he reminded himself, she was to be working here, and that might make things messy.

More than that, he still could not quite read those bright blue eyes.

And so he didn't tell her what he'd been about to say and went for the safer option instead. 'It might help you get a feel for the place. Flamenco is a way of life here.'

'Then I'll think about it.' She gave him a smile. 'Goodnight.' She dug in her purse to retrieve the key, then clearly remembered where she was, and felt that she should make some effort. 'Rather, *buenas noches*.'

'Goodnight, Emily,' he responded in English, pushing open the heavy gate. She wasn't sure if it was a little rebuke as to how dreadful her rusty Spanish was, but as she turned to the door he added, *'Que tengas dulces sueños.'*

Emily didn't translate it—she just looked at her shaky hands as she heard the gate close behind him. She walked away and turned the key in the apartment door and let herself in, hearing his footsteps as he walked to his own residence.

It wasn't so much a relief to close the door. It felt more as if she'd achieved an impossible feat.

One more second and she'd possibly have been an English girl behaving badly abroad.

And yet he'd done nothing…said nothing untoward. He'd been utterly polite and nice.

With an edge.

There had been a sharp sensual edge to him that she'd never glimpsed in another, let alone herself.

Taking her shoes off provided no relief—even though it should have, given that her feet had been agony since Heathrow.

Even taking her bra off did not elicit the usual exhalation of pleasure. Her breasts felt as constricted as if she was still wearing it, and her knickers were damp as she slid them off.

She was more aware of her body than she'd ever been.

The bathroom was white, with a huge dome-shaped showerhead that she hurried to stand under. And it was so nice that she didn't even have to dig through her suitcase to find toiletries—they were all there on display, in striking cut glass bottles that she was careful not to drop.

She opened one of the stoppers and took a breath of body wash. But, as decadent and delicious as it was, the scent wasn't his.

Emily washed quickly and wrapped herself in a very

soft towel. And then, trying to ignore her thrumming body, she took herself to a very vast bed, with white sheets tucked so tightly in it took her a moment to realise she wasn't under the top one.

Gosh.

She'd left the shutters open earlier, and the sound from outside was one of a breezy cool night and a city as close to asleep as the centre of a city ever came. She got up to close them, but then changed her mind and left them. She found the jagged piece of amber resin and placed it by her bedside light. She gazed at it as she lay there, naked in bed for the first time in her life.

Let me out, the little butterfly wing seemed to say.

Not yet, Emily thought. Because her holiday romance had its allocated slot in six weeks' time... And she doubted it would be with anyone as thrilling or beautiful as Alejandro Romero.

He was probably like that with everyone, Emily warned herself. He no doubt smiled that decadent smile to all and sundry. She thought of the lipstick on the edge of his mouth. Although it had faded by the end of the night, some had remained, as if serving as a warning.

Alejandro had surely just been being polite to a newcomer, Emily decided, confused by the tears suddenly in her eyes. But it was more than a little sad that at the age of twenty-six, without a touch or a kiss, somehow this had been the most wonderful night of her life.

Only as she started to drift off did she allow herself to dwell on his words.

'Que tengas dulces sueños.'—*'Have sweet dreams.'*
Emily dared not.

CHAPTER FOUR

EVEN IN HER very unfamiliar surroundings, Emily woke to a familiar headspace.

Common sense had returned, and all attempts at flights of fancy had been safely battened down.

Her new boss had simply been being perfectly nice.

Selecting a pale grey top to go with a fresh pair of black trousers—more stretchy ones that looked as if they had a belt and pockets but were really just yoga pants in disguise—she dressed, then slipped on some comfortable flats.

After tying her hair back in a low ponytail she was ready to face the day, and slipped out of the apartment with her camera.

It was early, but she wanted to get a feel for the place while it was quiet.

Gosh, it was gorgeous.

She took a couple of shots of the courtyard, and then looked over at a row of archways and saw black barrels, neatly stacked. But really it was the light that caught her attention. She took a few more shots, capturing the morning sun streaming through the high, round, stained glass windows in each archway.

Making her way down past the archways, she saw

that there were many of them, and it dawned on her just how immense and magnificent the bodega was.

And then she saw him.

Alejandro.

She had thought he would be in an office, or still sleeping, but he was there, in an archway, leaning over a barrel.

She took a few shots of him.

'Hey!' Alejandro said, straightening up.

'Sorry,' Emily said. 'I was just…' She felt as if she'd been caught staring. 'I wanted some natural shots.'

'Don't be sorry.' He shrugged. 'It's good that you're straight on to it. We want the website up and running as soon as we can. But it has to be right…'

'The light's beautiful in here.'

'And brief,' he said. 'In summer that's important, or it would get far too hot, but by eight the sun has moved on and internal lights come on for the tastings.'

'So, this is where the product is stored…?'

'And aged.' He nodded. 'The barrels are moved… rotated.'

'Is that what you were doing?'

He laughed.

'What's so funny?'

'I would like to say yes, but the truth is I was looking for a lost earring.'

'Oh.'

Last night she had thought he looked ready for work. This morning she saw him when he actually was.

His jaw was clean-shaven, his hair still damp, and for a moment she wished, honestly, that she was the woman whose earring he looked for.

Ridiculous!

She wasn't out of practice—she'd never even got as far as practising.

'Hola!'

Emily turned and saw the elusive Sophia, elegant in white. She felt fat and frumpy and just so unglamorous.

'I am so sorry about yesterday. My ankles…' Sophia turned to Alejandro. 'What are you doing in the bodega?' she asked him. 'I was going to give Emily a tour—I certainly didn't expect you to.' She turned to Emily. 'I really am sorry I wasn't there to greet you. But I've been ordered to rest, so you only have me for today.' She rolled her eyes. 'I have the most brilliant nanny, but unfortunately she can't do my bedrest for me.'

'You have a son?' Emily checked, but she knew because she'd seen pictures of him on social media. 'Pedro?'

'That's right—this little one is my second.' Sophia said, affectionately touching her bump. 'Pedro is going to be so jealous…'

'If you're going to talk babies,' Alejandro cut in, 'I am out of here. Sophia, can you see that Emily has a laptop and a phone?'

'I have my own…'

'Perhaps,' he said, 'but for your work here…' He looked over to Sophia. 'I'll leave it to you to explain.'

'Of course.' Sophia nodded. 'Actually, I'll go and get the laptop and files now. Perhaps we can have breakfast out here, Emily?'

'Sure.'

Sophia clipped off, in heels that defied her advanced pregnancy, but surprisingly for Emily, despite his clear declaration just a moment ago that he was leaving, Alejandro didn't.

'How are you?' he asked.

'Very well, thank you,' she replied rather formally. 'I enjoyed the tasting.'

'That's good,' he responded.

All the ease of last night seemed to have left them, and to Emily it felt like proof that she'd simply misread things. She felt embarrassed at the speed of her attraction to the first good-looking man to pay her attention—like some over-eager fangirl.

Only that wasn't quite true.

There had been good-looking guests at the B&B—though admittedly not as divine as Alejandro. And in her time at university she'd started to socialise and had even been chatted up a few times...

It was her reaction to *him* that bewildered her.

Desperate for something to say, she cast her gaze around and caught a glint of light between two heavy barrels.

'There it is.'

'What?'

'The earring,' she said, getting down on the sandy floor to retrieve it, relieved to have something to do rather than standing there awkwardly.

Only possibly it wasn't her best angle as, bottom in the air, she stretched her arm between the barrels.

'Got it...'

He offered his hand to help her up, but Emily chose to lean on one of the barrels. She looked at the gorgeous chandelier earring made of diamonds for a moment, and then looked back at him.

He said nothing, just held out a hand for the earring, and she dropped it into his palm, trying to avoid contact.

'Thank you,' he said, and pocketed it. His voice was

gravelly, and he cleared his throat and looked straight at her. 'What are we going to do, Emily?' he asked.

She was back in the path of his chocolate gaze and it simply melted her.

'I don't know,' she responded.

It was barely seven in the morning and she felt as turned on as she had last night, as full of desire as she had last night, but with one difference...

It was a very mutual desire.

Perhaps she only recognised it in him because she'd never seen it in another until now—pure, naked lust, aimed in her direction.

Nothing was said, their bodies did not touch, and there was no word she could think of to define the odd silence that filled the still space.

'Come here,' he said.

She took a step towards him and his gorgeous scent drew her another step closer.

'I wish I'd kissed you last night,' he said. 'I couldn't read you, though.'

And that was rare for Alejandro. He could feel their desire, he had seen she was turned on and felt the sensual swirl of the air, yet her eyes were darting and nervous, as if she was scared of something as nice as kissing.

Light fell on her face from the stained-glass window. 'You're gorgeous.'

'I'm really not,' Emily said.

'Oh, you really are.' He seemed to think about her words for a moment. 'Why would you say that?'

'Say what?'

'Why would you put yourself down? I gave you a compliment.'

She didn't know how to accept one, though. There really hadn't been many.

'You're gorgeous,' he repeated.

'Thank you,' she said, her cheeks flaming, and then she added, 'So are you.'

'Thank you,' he said. 'For the record, I never get involved with anyone at work…'

'Liar…' She smiled.

'No!' He shook his head, but then must have reconsidered that statement. 'Oh, Sophia and I were an item ages ago, long before she worked for me.'

Oh, God! He was so worldly, and he was so confident, and everything she was not.

'But tonight,' Alejandro said, 'perhaps we…?'

She could take it no more. She raised herself onto tiptoe and placed her lips on his, just for a second, for one tiny taste.

'Hey!'

He pulled back and she stood there, mortified by her own boldness and appalled at how she had misread things. But as she turned to flee, she felt his hands still on her hips, and it took her a second to register that he was smiling.

'I was going to say,' he said, 'that tonight perhaps we could meet and address things.'

It was not said in chastisement, because his tongue had bobbed out and tasted the place where her lips had been. 'However, I can't let you go after that…'

He lowered his head and his mouth came down on hers. Then he prised her lips open with his tongue.

It was a kiss she had hoped existed.

A kiss so thorough that she moaned into his mouth.

A kiss that just blocked out the sun and made the floor feel absent—as if she were floating.

This was how a kiss should be. She knew it because she'd found out how it felt to crave and to be craved.

His hands pressed into her bottom. His palms were hot through the fabric, and then decisive as he pulled her into his groin. The length and hardness of him pressed into her soft stomach felt indecent. Deliciously indecent and something she ached to explore.

His mouth moved to her neck and she was panting, a little dizzy as his hands slipped under her thin top.

There wasn't time to suck in her stomach—there wasn't even any thought that she ought to suck in her stomach. His hands were giving her flesh a light tickle on their way up to the underside of her breast...

'I love your breasts,' he said into her neck. 'I am going to love your breasts.'

And Emily loved his words, for they promised there would be more of this later.

He stroked her nipples through the lace of her bra and his lips were softer now, gliding back down, and she was grateful for his control. Especially when she heard the distant sound of footsteps, hating the sound of them, and they both pulled back.

For the first time in her life Emily had to make herself decent, pulling down her top. Even if it had been only a kiss, it was her first real one.

She felt as if they might have had sex against the barrels. As if, without his control, they jolly well could have.

'Discreción...' he warned, as if this was all new to him too.

'Still here?' Sophia said to Alejandro, and then she looked down and gave Emily a rather startled look.

Emily soon saw why—there was sawdust on her knees.

'Emily just found Mariana's earring…' said Alejandro.

'Oh!' Sophia said and then laughed as if at her own private joke—because *as if* the very shy and awkward Emily would be on her knees with Alejandro! 'Just as well. Mariana has just texted me, insisting that it be found.'

'See that she gets it.'

He handed the earring to Sophia, who replied in Spanish with a smirk, 'You have a very demanding fiancée, Alejandro.'

Unfortunately for Emily, she understood what had just been said.

Fiancée?

He was *engaged*!

Emily was still reeling from their kiss, and was now appalled by this new revelation—not that Sophia noticed.

'Breakfast?' she suggested.

'Of course,' Emily said, unable to look at Alejandro, her lips pinching together as they walked out to a courtyard table.

Just before Alejandro headed off Sophia told him she would take Emily to the vineyards that afternoon.

'I'll take her,' he said. 'You've already done enough by coming in this morning. You really need to get those feet up.'

'I know. They're like balloons.'

They really were not, Emily thought as she and Sophia took a seat at the table. What on earth would Alejandro say if he saw her feet, still swollen from the flight yesterday?

And then she smarted. No, he would not be seeing hers.

The courtyard was the perfect place to take breakfast, scented with the Seville orange trees, which were ripe with lush fruit, but Emily was too upset by what she'd just heard to really appreciate the gorgeous surroundings.

Sophia ordered hot chocolate and churros, and Emily said she would like the same.

She was frantically trying to turn her mind to work as Sophia went through the new phone and laptop with her, and explained that all her work must take place on these devices. The images she took inside the bodega over the next six weeks all belonged to the Romeros— they were dealing with liquid gold after all.

'Any new programs you need just speak with IT, but it's better for now that it's all on here.'

'Sure.'

The chocolate was thick and sweet and felt almost *necessary*—like hot sugary tea after a shock.

And Emily *was* shocked.

Not just that Alejandro was engaged to another woman, more at her own reckless behaviour. This was the biggest career break of her life, and yet there she'd been wrapped around Alejandro.

Sure, she wanted fun and romance—but after her six-week tenure, not twelve hours after landing.

And yet even if it would never be repeated, and should never have taken place, she did not know how to regret it, for it felt as if she'd glimpsed bliss.

'How is the accommodation?' Sophia asked as more hot chocolate was served.

'Wonderful!' Emily nodded. 'Although I admit, I was worried I was going to be sharing with the house-keeper...'

'God, we wouldn't do that to you! It's always vacant. Alejandro prefers that his staff live out. And it's just as well that they do—they would need to bleach their eyes otherwise.' Perhaps she saw Emily's frown. 'He has many lovers,' she explained.

'My mistake...' Emily did her best to sound casual '...but I thought you just said he was engaged.'

'Not formally engaged.' She rolled her eyes and made a wavering gesture with her hand. 'They're very on-off. He does what he chooses while Mariana waits impatiently in the wings. Or should I say soars overhead like a vulture, waiting for it to go wrong—as it invariably does...'

She pulled up a map onscreen that showed Emily the sherry triangle and the vineyards she would be going to visit today. A lot of the vineyards seemed to be the property of the Romeros.

'The Romeros want that part...' Sophia pointed to another area of the map. 'That's Mariana's family's land. When she and Alejandro marry the bodegas will merge.'

Emily's heart forced her to at least make an attempt at hope. '*If* they marry.'

'Oh, they'll marry,' Sophia said, with a certainty that made Emily's newly kissed lips pinch in tension. 'Both the families want it, and in fairness Mariana is probably the only person who could put up with one of the Romero brothers.'

'I see…'

'They're great to work for, though,' Sophia said. 'You just have to think product, product, product. Have you managed to do any research?'

'Not really,' Emily admitted. 'I tried, but the old website is down and I kept coming up with Maria de Luca…'

'Maria's their mother…' Sophia tapped away on the laptop that would soon be Emily's. 'Technically.'

'Technically?'

'She left José, their father.' She waved her hand in the air. 'Long ago…as soon as Carmen was born. She's a couple of years younger than me…so twenty-five years ago or more.' She leant forward and lowered her voice. 'But now Maria has decided to start visiting José…' She made a money gesture with her hands. 'No doubt she's trying to ensure that her name is in the will and her image remains on the bottle.'

'The woman on the label is their mother?' Emily checked, surprised that Alejandro hadn't mentioned it last night.

'*Sí.*' Sophia nodded. 'Maria's a very famous flamenco dancer—not just in Spain but internationally. Although she won't be attending the festival here! Believe me, she would get the cold shoulder. I'm only telling you this so when you read about who she is for yourself you don't decide to do a section on the website on her. It wouldn't go down well.'

Emily was very relieved to have the warning, because, knowing now that the gorgeous woman on the bottle was actually a legend in her own right, of *course* she would have gone down that road.

'Last year they started working on the rebranding. José wanted every trace of Maria gone, and of course Sebastián and Carmen agreed.'

'What about Alejandro?'

'He wanted her image to remain, but was outvoted,' she said. 'But then José got ill and suddenly changed his mind. Sebastián and Carmen want the new branding to go ahead, but it's Alejandro who has the deciding vote now.'

'So I'm to make no mention of her?' Emily frowned, because it seemed a rather large thing to leave out.

'I honestly don't know,' Sophia admitted. 'Sebastián is in Madrid at the moment, and then he's off to New York. He would rip her off every label if he could.' She shrugged, but more in exasperation than indifference. 'Just tread gently, and don't go planning anything on the website around her.'

'Thanks for the heads-up,' Emily said, and she sincerely meant it.

'You'll be fine. You'll be mainly dealing with Alejandro, and he doesn't let emotions get in the way...' She moved on to other matters. 'Most of the staff speak a little English, or at least enough to get by...'

'That's good.'

'But Alejandro says do your work in English, then we'll arrange translation. Just...' She paused. 'The other website design company we looked at was so...' She raised her hands in an exasperated gesture. 'No original ideas. So staid and boring...' She smiled. 'And the Romeros are not.'

Emily had rather worked that out for herself!

'If Sebastián closes this deal in NYC it will be huge. He wants the new website up as soon as possible. But Alejandro is more insistent on you taking the time to get it right...'

'What about the sister?'

'Carmen has very little to do with the bodega. She practically lives in the family stables.'

It was a very busy morning for Emily. She was shown the IT office, and she met the staff she'd be working with, and despite the ancient surroundings and furnishings it was all very high-tech.

She also found out, when they went for second breakfast—*second breakfast!*—that lunch was generally taken around three p.m., and that it was very normal in Spain to work through till eight.

'You're going to need every hour,' Sophia warned.

'I am,' Emily agreed.

At first six weeks had seemed plenty of time, but there was so much to take in and find out.

And to avoid!

'The brothers' offices are at the top,' Sophia said, as they stood at the bottom of a very grand staircase. 'But I for one am not up to climbing four flights of stairs.'

'There's no elevator?'

'No. And really there's no need to go up there. Most meetings are held in the courtyard or online, as the brothers are rarely here. Sebastián spends a lot of time in Madrid, and Alejandro is all over the place—often in Seville.' She looked up. 'Here he is now.'

Indeed he was—coming down the stairs and carrying his jacket. He looked busy, and as if a trip to the vineyards was the last thing he needed right now.

* * *

'I'm fine to take Emily,' Sophia told him in Spanish.

'It's okay,' he said. 'I do appreciate you coming in. But go home. I can take it from here.'

Of course Alejandro didn't add that he *wanted* to take it from here.

He knew that Emily deserved some sort of an explanation.

Actually, so did he. Alejandro had been doing a little research of his own, and had taken a closer look at the website for the bed and breakfast she ran...

It would seem Emily Jacobs might have a few secrets of her own!

CHAPTER FIVE

'DO YOU NEED to collect anything?' Alejandro asked.

'My tripod and such…'

'Sure.' He nodded. 'Sophia, could you have Jorge bring my car?'

'Don't you want him to drive?' Sophia checked, but Alejandro shook his head.

'No need.'

Jorge helped Emily with her equipment, and as he loaded it into the boot Emily got into the passenger side. Alejandro sat, engine idling, strumming his fingers on the steering wheel. It was a very low car—so much so that she was actually pleased with her sensible trousers.

'Thanks for this,' Emily said as they pulled out of the bodega. 'Though I'd have been happy to go and explore by myself.'

'You know about sherry production, then?' he said, and glanced over as Emily fought not to curl her lip. 'It's not a leisure trip.'

'Of course not.'

He manoeuvred the silver car easily through the traffic, telling her it was mainly one-way.

'How was Sophia?' he asked.

'Very helpful,' Emily responded, wishing he would address what had been said earlier, but he did not.

Instead, as they left the city behind them, he glanced over. 'Is this what you look like when you're sulking?'

She didn't answer straight away, but pulled the sun visor down and looked at her pale, pinched reflection in the mirror. 'This is what I look like most of the time.' It was an honest answer, and she closed the shade and went back to looking out of the window. But then she did tell him how she was feeling. 'I would never have kissed you if I'd known you were engaged to someone else.'

'No, you wouldn't have, would you?' he said, glancing over and getting a view of the back of her head.

They drove through rolling hills filled with bare vines and instead of telling her about the different grapes, and pointing out the Romero territories, for once Alejandro was unsure what to say.

'Emily...' he began.

'Yes?' she responded, without looking at him, and after a couple more moments of silence he pulled over.

'Emily,' he said again, and now she looked at him.

He looked at her blue eyes and saw the sparkle of tears in them. They were not unexpected, he thought, when perhaps they should be?

It moved him in an unexpected way. It moved him that this nice, shy, funny, awkward woman did not want to have kissed a man who was engaged to someone else, and he could not fault that.

He could tease her, though.

'It was just a kiss.'

'That should never have taken place.'

She made it sound as if they'd spent a month locked away having torrid sex, rather than sharing a slow morning kiss.

Yet her reaction endeared her to him, and as she went to open the car door Alejandro realised he'd better stop teasing, and caught her arm.

'I was joking.'

She put her bottom back on the seat and he leant over and closed the car door.

'I don't often joke,' he said. 'Perhaps because I'm not very good at it.' He looked at her burning cheeks. 'It was a lovely kiss and you have nothing to feel guilty about.'

He paused for a second.

'If I tell you something, can I ask that it goes no further?'

Emily's eyes darted. Should she say no? It was surely too soon for secrets? She was only just emerging from layers of lies. But then she looked back to his gaze and could see that this very suave man was undecided, almost tentative, possibly as confused as she.

And so she nodded.

'It's complicated,' he said.

'Please—just be honest.'

'Mariana and I broke up at Christmas.'

'No...' She was so sick of being lied to that she was braver than she thought she could be. She put a hand up to his clean-shaven jaw and with her finger brushed the exact spot where the lipstick had been last night. 'So it wasn't Mariana's lipstick you were wearing last night?'

'It was.' He nodded. 'For the last six weeks I've tried to keep up the pretence—because just after Christmas we found out that my father is very ill. He wants our marriage to take place before he dies. But I just can't keep up the pretence any longer.'

'Why start it in the first place?'

'I didn't start it—I was practically born into it. It's all about old legacies and promises. The land belonging to Mariana's family is relatively small, but it is rich and productive and has long been fought over. If another buyer came in, or another bodega merged with it...' He shrugged. 'My family have long since wanted that land. Mariana's father and mine came to an agreement, and it's something we've grown up with. The golden couple in the golden sherry triangle. But I just came to realise that it wasn't for me. I don't want marriage. I'm not even a man to date long-term...'

'I had already worked that out,' Emily said. 'But don't lie, please.'

'I won't. If you're looking for a relationship, don't look to me.'

She realised he was actually being breathtakingly honest.

Alejandro started the car's engine and indicated to pull out, but before he did he asked a question of his own. 'What about *your* fiancé?'

'Touché...' Emily begrudgingly smiled. 'How do you know about Gordon?'

'I looked you up.'

Late last night—or rather early that morning—his curiosity had been piqued. Something that rarely happened. It had taken him ages to find Emily—her business was very new.

He'd seen a lovely family-run business, the happy couple, their smiles for the cameras... But Alejandro had noticed how the man's arm was held so awkwardly around Emily, and the tension in her features…

He'd also realised that her dreadful hair hadn't been caused by some recent ghastly slip of the hairdresser's scissors—she'd worn it like that for years.

He glanced over at her curls when she remained silent.

'We broke up three months ago,' she finally admitted.

'Good,' he said.

'Most people offer their commiserations.'

'Good for them.' Alejandro shrugged. 'So, you owned a business together?'

'No…' Emily swallowed. 'It was his mother's business. She died a few months ago. He broke things off shortly after.'

'Why?'

She sucked in her breath at his question.

'Well, I need to know,' Alejandro said. 'If I'm in the running to be your rebound guy, I have to know what issues to work on.'

He'd brought a reluctant smile to her lips, but it was fleeting.

'Couldn't you afford to buy him out?' he asked.

'It was only his.'

'Emily…' he said in reproach. 'Don't tell me you didn't get your name on a contract…'

'I didn't.'

He tutted.

'I didn't want a messy break-up. You know how hard these things are.'

'No.' He shook his head and said what few people

would. 'Breaking up doesn't have to be hard. I do it all the time...' He smiled at her. 'I mean, I do it a lot!'

'I'm sure sometimes it hurts more than most.'

'No.' He would not be swayed. 'I used to say it to my parents when they fought: why do you have to make things so complicated? You love to be with the other? Stay. You don't love to be with the other? Then go. Why do you have to make all this drama between you?'

'Did they fight a lot?'

'A *lot*,' he agreed. 'My mother is a very flamenco talented dancer. Maria de Luca.'

'I don't really know much about flamenco...'

He liked their slow conversation...a few kilometres, a few words, a stretch of silence as they both thought over what the other had said.

'You're unacquainted with it,' he said. 'Is that the right word?'

'Maybe...'

She felt unacquainted with so many things.

'I'd like to see the equestrian school in Jerez,' she told him. 'I'd never heard about the dancing horses before.'

'My sister Carmen is into all that.' He nodded. 'I'll set up a meeting with her.'

A few more kilometres passed. He hadn't driven with such gentle company in as long as he could remember.

'Do you have brothers or sisters?' Alejandro asked.

'No.' Emily shook her head. 'But I have a friend, Anna, and I consider her to be a sister. We grew up together...'

'What about your parents?'

'They're both dead.'

He looked over at her and on this occasion he did commiserate. 'I'm sorry.'

'Thank you.'

'Recently?'

'Not really. My mother died during my final year at university—that's why I dropped out. My father had dementia. He died three years ago…'

'You dropped out to care for him?'

'Yes.'

'That must have been difficult.' He glanced over again. 'Or am I saying the wrong thing?'

'No, it *was* very difficult,' she admitted. 'I still don't know if it was the right thing to do. My mother asked me not to let him go into care, and I felt I had to keep that promise, but…'

'I get it,' he said. 'Well, not exactly. But my father is…' He stared ahead as he drove. 'As I told you, he's not well.'

'I'm very sorry.'

'Well, there's life in him yet, and he too is trying to push for…' He waved his hand in frustration at the limits of his English. 'I can talk business in English, but…' He thought for a moment. 'He uses emotion.' Alejandro glanced over at Emily. 'Did Sophia tell you about the rebranding?'

'She mentioned something…' Emily said.

'Well, you'll know that my father now wants my mother's picture to remain on our label.'

'I'm sure whatever you choose will be right.'

He smiled to himself as she shifted a little in her seat, clearly choosing her words carefully.

God, she was sweet. The least confrontational person he'd ever met. So much so, that she pressed a random button, perhaps in the hope of winding down the window, just for something to do rather than discuss the verboten subject of his mother.

'Why are you putting the child locks on?' he teased, and she laughed.

'Caught!'

She was nervous—he could tell. 'Sophia told you to stay away from it?'

She nodded. 'But I don't see how I can. I want a website that pleases everyone. Your father included…'

'Let me discuss it with my brother and sister.'

'Of course.'

Alejandro was used to playing hardball, and he liked her gentle take on things. He'd never spoken so easily to another person, or listened so carefully…

'Are you proud of your mother?' she asked.

'Yes,' he said. His response was immediate, and surprised even himself—he'd never been allowed to admit being proud of his mother to anyone. Emily was the first person in for ever who had referred to his mother's talent. 'I used to go backstage with her and I could hear the cheers. She is incredibly talented.'

'I'd love to have learned to dance.'

'You didn't?'

'I started ballet, but…'

'But?'

'I hated it.' She sighed at the memory. 'One of the other girls called me fat…'

'*Were* you fat?'

'A bit.'

'We call fat kids cute here…' he said. 'My sister was very "cute",' he said, and made her laugh. 'Now she's a brilliant equestrian.' He slowed the car down. 'This is our family residence.'

She looked at a huge gated property and saw, in the distance, a sprawling hacienda. 'That's your home?'

'It was. See the stables? That's where Carmen spends most of her time.'

'She lives here with your father?'

'Yes,' Alejandro said. 'When she's not practising in the arena here, she's at the equestrian school. It's a kind of horse ballet...' he said, in an attempt to describe it.

'Dressage?'

'A form of it, but really quite incredible. It's a big part of life here in Jerez. Carmen could ride before she could walk.'

'She didn't take up flamenco?'

'God, no, she hates it.'

And for years so had he. But last night, watching Emily's rapt expression, he had found his pleasure in it starting to return...

'What was it like having a famous mother?'

When he didn't answer Emily corrected herself.

'Of course she'd have just been your mum...'

'Oh, no,' he said. 'She was the star at home, believe me. Always she wanted to be on tour or performing. My father was jealous—he wanted her to be at home more. Instead, we had nannies. And every time she came home there was another argument. So, of course, she stopped coming home...'

Alejandro had surprised Emily. She'd expected bitterness—but, no, he seemed to see both sides.

'If your fiancé had asked you to stop working...'

'Oh, he never would have—he *loved* me working,'

Emily said, and that made them both laugh. Then she was serious. 'So long as it was in *his* business.'

'You know, you could probably contest his ownership of it. I mean if you were together all these years you could argue you had a verbal contract...'

'No.' Emily shook her head. 'I mean, I know I could fight it—but what's the point? Lesson well and truly learnt. I'll never get involved with someone who has a family business again...'

She halted, aware of what she'd just said, but Alejandro just laughed at her discomfort.

'Good,' he said. 'Because I don't do involved relationships.' Then he was serious too. 'You say he liked you working?'

'Yes, but he'd never have supported me in my own venture.'

'That's sad.'

'Is it?'

'Yes,' Alejandro said. 'I've seen the results of that first-hand. If my father had gone and watched my mother, travelled with her...'

'Well, he did have three children.'

'We'd have been raised by nannies either way.' He looked over to her. 'Like I said before, break-ups don't have to be hard. People just make them so.'

'I think it depends on if you're the one doing the breaking up—'

'No,' he cut in. 'Why not just agree from the start that it goes nowhere? Enjoy each other for however long and then walk away without regret?'

Alejandro had made it sound like an invitation...as if he was inviting himself on her adventure.

They drove in silence but the words hung between

them and she played them over and over, wondering if by some chance he'd been talking about them.

He made it sound so easy…so uncomplicated.

Could it be?

CHAPTER SIX

THE BARE VINES seemed endless, and the sun was low in the late-afternoon sky as they pulled in at a vineyard.

'In summer this is busy,' said Alejandro. 'But now we have just select groups—fine dining for suppliers and exporters, weddings and such…'

He took her up to the function room, where they spoke with the head chef, who seemed a little startled to see Alejandro.

'It's fine,' he said, 'we're not here to eat. I'm just showing Emily around. She's designing the new website. Here we hold weddings, and the annual Romero ball,' he told her.

'I've heard about that.'

'It's stunning when it's lit up for the evening.'

'I'd love to see it.'

'Would you?'

She nodded.

'We're only open for lunches at the moment,' the chef explained. 'Perhaps come back at the weekend?'

They sorted out times, then headed down to the ground floor, where there were just a few staff around. They all smiled at Alejandro and nodded to Emily, as she stood taking frantic notes and the odd photo.

'This is Carlos,' he said, introducing her to one of the staff. 'I'll leave Emily with you for a moment,' he told him. 'Carlos is the person to ask for all historical details and the family tree...'

Carlos was indeed knowledgeable, and took her to the vast presses where the grapes were crushed. The walls were lined with images of days gone by, when it had been done by foot. She looked at the photos of men pushing the grapes barefoot.

'It was a celebration,' Carlos explained. 'One basket per man...one bottle of sherry for a basket.' He took her outside. 'This is where the chickens used to be kept.'

'A lot of chickens,' Emily said.

Alejandro returned then and took over.

'They used to use egg whites to clarify the sherry,' he told her, and Emily honestly considered recording him, because she could barely keep up with her notes.

Still, it might be better not to, as his voice was so utterly delicious. She'd end up being lost in a daydream rather than getting on with her work.

'It's so beautiful here,' she said as they walked through the vineyards.

The wind was biting, and it was the first time she'd been cold since arriving in Jerez. Only it felt nice being cold with him...

'The staff have all gone.'

'How do you know?'

'Carlos always leaves last...' He pointed to a motorbike threading its way through the hills.

He turned her to face him and she felt relief to be alone with him.

'We'll head back soon,' he said. 'But first...'

And he resumed the kiss almost where they had left it that morning, but with even deeper feeling now.

Alejandro had never held anyone so soft before. He could not get enough of her shapely body.

The bite of the wind was soon forgotten, and even more so when they sank down onto the ground.

'We're going to have to dust each other off,' Alejandro said, his hand slipping inside her top and, with no chance of being disturbed now, unhooking her bra.

'Not here...' she whispered, all the while kissing him back.

'Of course not,' he said, stroking her breast as she lay back beneath the bliss of him. 'I'm taking you home to bed...'

And somewhere during that journey she knew she would have to tell him her truth.

He was half on top of her, lifting her top so that her breast was exposed to the cool evening air, and she bit on her lip as he held her breast and took it in his mouth.

'I told you I would love your breasts.'

She loved his detailed exploration.

He was bruising her with his mouth, she was certain of it, but she was impatient for more, and his busy tongue meant that his hand was free to slip down.

'Alejandro...'

She closed her eyes as his fingers slipped further, to where she was slick and warm, and she knew she had to tell him that she'd never done even a tenth of this before.

And it was at that moment Emily found out the true temptation of sex—because his finger seemed to meet her epicentre.

'Shh…' he said, silencing her faint protests that she had something to tell him. 'Just relax…'

'I want to…'

'Then do.'

The sky was purple and pink and fringed with orange, and his mouth was back on her tender breast as his fingers stroked her, not so slowly now.

'God…'

He could feel her trembling, and the little choking sounds she made had his stomach tightening.

She was fighting with herself, Alejandro realised, and assumed it was some kind of girly guilt after the awful Gordon that was holding her back.

'Do you want me to stop?'

'No, never stop…'

They were just kissing, just touching, but he seemed to be aching for her intimate touch too, because he took her hand and she felt him hard beneath her palm. It excited her—ridiculously so.

He was taking her to a place that she had only ever glimpsed…that no reluctant bland kiss from Gordon had ever taken her to.

He kissed her tense mouth, coaxing her to relax with both his hand and his tongue, and he was so turned on himself, so completely turned on, that he made one straightforward request.

'Take it out,' he said, his voice hoarse. He was so turned on at the feel of her bottom lifting and her thighs tightening on his hand. 'Or I'm going to climax.'

Her hands went for his belt and he closed his eyes

in frustration, because he was right on the edge. So he took over. Taking himself out so that he was over her hip. Then his hand returned to the slipperiest, sweetest place.

He had brought her out here for a kiss, but had somehow hurtled back to his teenage years and forbidden gropes among the vines, and he had never enjoyed it more.

The lights went on then. The whole winery lit up and her eyes opened in shock.

He smothered her anguished cry.

'I arranged it,' he told her. 'Don't worry, it's just us here…'

It wasn't just the lights…it was the pressure of his fingers as they buried themselves in her that had caused her to cry out when the lights had come on.

She reached for him, dared to touch him, surprised by the soft skin and the steel beneath. The feel of his wet tip on her palm spread a delicious warmth through her, and finally she was caving in rather than fighting…

The sight of her clenched jaw and compressed lips, the sounds she made, brought Alejandro a pleasure so pure that if he'd been able to tear his hand away he'd have stroked out his own climax. But instead he leant up on his elbow, feeling the last flickers or her orgasm, and watching with pleasure as her parted lips spread into a smile that felt as if it was only for him.

'Nice?' he asked as her smile faded.

'So nice…'

He rolled on top of her and his erection lay between

them. He looked down at her. 'I only brought you out here to see the lights.'

'Please!'

'I'm serious.' He smiled. 'A kiss, maybe, but...' He was rocking a little, staring down at her. The feel of her skin was bliss. 'I thought I was past sex outdoors... But maybe I'm not,' he said.

He wanted more of her secret smile, but her knees had come up enough so that she gripped him loosely, and now she leant up on her elbows.

'Not here,' Emily said again. His fingers had hurt enough for her to know she could not get away without telling him.

If only she knew how she'd have happily used her mouth, or her hand, because she could feel not just his erection but his whole body, taut and turned on. A little as she had felt in the seconds before her first orgasm... drawn towards pure pleasure.

He moved back and his erection sprang free. As he moved to get off her it brushed at her most intimate core, and he held the base as if it was some heat-seeking missile as it nudged her entrance.

She was still raw from coming, and yet so desperate for more.

'Alejandro, I've never...'

'I know,' he said. 'We'll go home.'

He rolled off and was unabashed as he lay on his back and tried to tuck his erection into black silk boxers.

She pulled up her knickers and trousers.

'I've never orgasmed before...' she said.

He turned his head and looked at her.

'I've never done anything...'

'What are you talking about?'

'I've never slept with anyone...'

'What?' He frowned. 'But you lived with your fiancé...'

'We had separate bedrooms.' She wanted to run away, but there really wasn't any point, given they were miles from anywhere and he was the one with the car. 'He said it was for religious reasons, and I accepted that.'

'Look I'm a good Catholic boy, well-lapsed, and it never stopped me...' Then he stopped joking. 'Are you serious?'

'Yes, but it doesn't have to change things. I mean, just because I've never...'

'You're telling me that you're a virgin?'

'Please don't make it sound like an ailment...'

'No.' He shook his head. 'No, it's more a...'

He tried to think of a more suitable word, but where Alejandro was concerned possibly she'd chosen right.

'Emily, it changes a lot of things. Look, I want you, but I don't want...' How best to say it? 'I think if you've waited this long, why throw it away on someone who...?' He was trying to be honest. 'It makes sense now.'

'What does?'

'We were so hot for each other last night...we should have ended up in bed.'

'So, you'd have been fine if it had just been a pick-up in a bar?'

'What's wrong with that?'

'Everything.'

'See?' he said gently. 'You do want more.'

* * *

'I'd want more than one night,' she admitted, surprising herself with how, even on such a personal topic, she found it easy to be honest with him. 'Gosh, can't I have a little romance with my sex, please? I'm not asking for life…'

'Emily…' He looked into her eyes and with clear regret shook his head. 'I don't do romance.'

She would have liked to refute that, because as he helped her up they stood under the lights that he'd arranged to be turned on just for her. And under the starry Jerez night, he was kind…

It was the most romance she had ever known.

It was a horrible walk back to the car.

There, he dusted them off. He even kept one of those lint rollers in the car.

'Do you keep one handy for all the times you take virgins out into the Romero vineyards?' she asked.

He didn't laugh at her joke—just brushed himself down and very neatly did up his tie.

Then there was the long journey home.

Not unpleasant…not tense.

They just talked about work, and the odd cloud formation, and how there were more nails in professional dancers' flamenco shoes than the cheaper ones.

An exchange of information, really, rather than conversation.

Or conversation, rather than talking.

'Thanks for the tour,' Emily said, and got out of the car, after he'd stopped at the front of the bodega.

But of course Alejandro didn't have to do things like go and park his car, so he got out too, and gave his keys to the security officer, and soon caught up with her as she punched in the code to his residence.

'You remembered,' he said.

'I did.'

She walked ahead of him on the steps, and took out the massive key as she did so. This time there was no lounging at the gates by Alejandro—just a brief goodnight.

Then, 'Emily?' he said as she turned the key.

'What?' she responded rather rudely, without turning around.

Because if she faced him then she might start crying. She could still feel their attraction, and it felt unfair that Alejandro wanted her, yet refused to give in to that want.

'I'm a bastard where women are concerned,' he said.

'I had heard.'

And she wished—how she wished—that he was just a little bit more of a bastard.

And would take her to bed.

She entered her apartment alone and sat in the dark on her sofa, wondering how long she might remain unwanted.

The glimpse of sex he'd shown her tonight had far from sated her…it had just made her more desirous, if that were possible.

Only it wasn't just sex she wanted to discover now.

She wanted *him*.

Well, no more!

A sound had her moving to the balcony. She saw a group of women, crossing the road, walking together and laughing, clapping as they walked.

A couple of other women were calling to them and

they turned. Emily looked to where they had come from, and it appeared to be a bar or a café. But then her eyes were drawn to the lit rooms above.

A dance school.

She thought of what Alejandro had said about taking lessons. Her!

He was a nice bastard…

She niggled him. Not at his conscience, because he was certain he'd done the right thing by her, but she just niggled him in a way no one else ever had.

Their attraction had been instant and undeniable, but it was more than that. He'd enjoyed last night. All the things that were so normal…the sherry-tasting, the *taberna*—had been made special.

The music, which he usually kept as background noise in his mind, had come forward. She'd made him laugh, and he didn't do much of that.

He hated it that he'd rejected her—especially given what she'd told him about her ex. Yet at the same time he knew his own reputation.

And a kind and gentle twenty-six-year-old virgin did not need his casual ways.

He loathed closeness.

Intimacy.

Drama and emotion.

Sex was just sex. He never mixed up the two…

And a holiday romance? Not a chance.

CHAPTER SEVEN

ALEJANDRO ENTERED EMILY'S temporary office, which overlooked the courtyard, the next morning.

'Are you okay?' he asked.

'Of course.'

Actually, she was all frazzled, and feeling frumpy in fresh black trousers and a navy top. And, yes, she knew the two didn't go together, but she'd thought they were both black when she'd dressed.

'Well, apart from the fact that Spanish water hates me.' She ran a finger through her curls, which had gone frothy at the ends, like cotton wool balls. 'What's the Spanish for hair conditioner?'

'Acondicionador de cabello.' Alejandro smiled. 'Just go to a salon…there's an excellent one in the *plaza*, or you can go to Calle Larga…'

'No need for that,' Emily said. 'I do my own hair.'

Alejandro, possibly wisely, chose not to comment. He knew she was just making small talk and trying to steer things back to normal between them.

The trouble was, things had *never* been normal between them.

Bad hair day or not, he was still strongly attracted to her, and he hated it that he'd made things so awkward.

'I'm trying to do the right thing,' he said, and took a seat on the edge of the desk. 'I *know* I'm doing the right thing.'

'Good for you,' Emily snapped, surprised at her own cheek, but she fervently disagreed.

She could think of nothing better than Alejandro being her first lover. Still, she wouldn't be telling him that, so she mustered her pride.

'It's fine, I'm over not having sex with you.' She gave a tight smile. 'I think I seem to go for men who don't want me.'

'Don't say that.'

'I'm joking,' Emily said. 'Sort of.'

She turned the conversation in the direction of work. It was the reason she was here, after all, and she did admire him for coming down and checking in on her.

'I really do need to know if I can mention your mother…'

'Leave it for now,' he said. 'Just work around it.'

'I'll do my best.' Emily nodded. 'I think I've got an idea about the website design. Do you have a moment?'

'Sure.'

'I found this photo…' She pulled up an image on her screen and he came and stood behind her. It was an image of a man rolling one of the beautiful old barrels, taken probably some fifty or so years ago.

'It's from the old website…' he said.

'I know that,' she responded, a little indignantly. 'But look.' She pulled up the image she'd taken of Alejandro yesterday morning, when he hadn't known she was there.

It was almost the same image.

Except with a modern take.

In the photograph, Alejandro's phone was sticking out of his back pocket, and his black trousers and white shirt were far more fitted than the clothes worn by the man in the old photograph. And with his hair and his designer stubble…? God, a model might have been hired for a week and this shot would never have looked better.

'That's really good.'

'Thank you,' Emily said, wondering if he was admiring her work or himself…but it didn't matter.

'I thought if we ran with some timeless images… how some things change but others stay the same…'

'I like it,' he said. 'Yes, I think it's just fresh enough without trying too hard.'

'I won't mention in the caption that you were looking for a diamond earring…'

'No.'

He looked at her then, wincing a little when he saw her red eyes, knowing he'd embarrassed and hurt her when it was the very last thing he'd wanted to do.

'Are you sure you're okay?' he asked.

'I will be.' She gave him a tight smile. 'Don't worry, Alejandro, I'm sure you're not that unique.'

She saw his eyes narrow a little, but he did not rise to the provocative threat, just shrugged one shoulder and had the gall to wish her well.

For the rest of her first week she saw him just a little, here and there.

His office was several flights up, so there was no

bumping into each other in the corridors. And despite their living next door to each other their paths only crossed once, in the early hours of morning as she lay on the ground in the courtyard.

She'd headed out to catch the sunrise, and before that she wanted to attempt to capture the moon as it drifted over the empty vines that knotted and weaved their way above the courtyard.

'Heavy night?' Alejandro asked, standing over her.

She had heard his footsteps but refused to acknowledge them. Now he stood looking down at her and making a dry joke, as if he'd found her passed out drunk in the courtyard.

'No,' she said, looking up and resisting saying that the heavy night had clearly been his.

She'd fallen into bed at ten, whereas Alejandro was clearly just getting home from a club, or a casino, or wherever his chosen venue for decadence had been that night. He was unshaven and dressed in a dark suit, his tie undone. Yet he looked so utterly perfect he somehow evoked the image of a movie star from decades ago.

She wasn't embarrassed to be caught lying down in an attempt to capture the perfect shot—simply grateful that she wasn't facing him in the small hours with some glamorous beauty on his arm.

'What are you doing, Emily?'

'I think these vines will be a beautiful border or background for the website. I'm done now...' She moved to get up, and when he offered his hand to help her stand, unthinkingly she took it.

Thinkingly their fingers remained laced together... like the vines she had just captured.

'Are you going back to bed now?' he asked, and

she was confused by the slightly suggestive tone to his voice. Confused that he could so coldly reject her and still so easily turn her on.

'No.' Emily removed her hand from his. 'I'm actually heading off to the vineyards. I thought I'd try for a sunrise shot.'

'Sounds good.' His voice was husky and he cleared his throat. 'I'm sure it will look amazing…'

'I hope so,' Emily said, and walked over to the steps, where all her equipment was stacked, waiting for her driver to arrive.

He watched as she packed up her beloved camera.

For Alejandro it had been a long night, moving from private club to private party in Seville—one of the hottest spots in Europe for night-life.

It had just not felt like it last night.

Now he knew why.

It was Emily's curves he wanted, her wild blonde curls in his fingers, and to know again the passion that smouldered untapped just beneath her uptight surface.

'Let me help you…' he offered, though really it was just to prolong their encounter.

But she refused his offer.

'No, thank you,' she responded with a tart edge—it clearly wasn't his chivalry she wanted.

He was trying to be the sensible one, but he was starting to wonder why he was bothering when it seemed neither of them really wanted him to be.

Emily most certainly didn't.

She sat bundled in a blanket in the middle of the vineyard and watched the sky turn a pale gold. It was rather a pale sunrise, compared to the violets and pinks of the sunset she'd witnessed before.

But she'd been with Alejandro then, Emily thought, and he made everything more beautiful, more vivid, somehow.

She kept telling herself to let it go. Only she was stuck in a loop, thinking of all the things he'd said that had made her laugh. His little teases and his easy acceptance of her...his sensual kisses and how he'd made her feel incredible when she was in his arms...

Enough! Emily decided as she packed up her equipment.

She was moving on from Alejandro Romero.

And that started today.

Flamenco Workshop... Flamenco for Beginners...

Alejandro had been right. It was everywhere. The shops even had flamenco shoes in baskets at the front, in red, purple, black... Turning them over, she saw there were nails banged into the heels and tips. Flamenco dresses ranged from a couple of euros up into the thousands.

Gosh, it was all so beautiful. There were even flamenco outfits for sale in the supermarkets.

It really was a way of life here.

And she wanted to taste it for herself.

If coming to Jerez was the bravest thing she had done in her life, then walking up the stone stairs and entering the doors of Eva's flamenco studio came a very close second.

Emily was one burning blush as she stood there in front of the very glamorous Eva, who was clearly on her lunch break. She was lying on a chaise longue, eating a sliced-up apple, but she smiled warmly as Emily entered.

'*Hola...*'

'I saw you perform on Sunday night,' Emily said in faltering Spanish. 'And I heard there were flamenco lessons… I was wondering if you do individual classes.' She couldn't bear the thought of dancing in a group—imagining she'd make an utter fool of herself in front of the locals. 'I mean, I'm…'

'*Claro que sí!*'—'*Of course!*' The woman smiled. 'But it is more enjoyable, as well as cheaper, to be in a group. This is my busy time, though, and unfortunately I am booked up.'

'That's fine,' Emily said. 'Alejandro just mentioned…'

'Alejandro sent you!' Eva exclaimed, and clearly that changed everything. 'Then of course I can make room for you.'

Her blush would not fade but Emily smiled at Eva's kind eyes.

'Come through. I'll show you around.'

The studio was mirrored, with wooden floors and silk shawls hanging over dividers, and rows of flamenco shoes all neatly placed in a corner.

'I really have no idea about flamenco,' Emily admitted.

'That is why you will take a beginners' class. I have a group booking at two, so we have some time now. Perhaps…?'

Emily was about to point out that she had to go back at work, but then thought that, in a way, this *was* work.

'I haven't got any shoes…'

'Soon,' Eva said. 'Wait until you have had a couple

of lessons before you spend your money. The first lesson is free…' She tapped her fingers into her palm and that incredible, precise sound was made again.

'That clapping…'

'It is called *palmas*,' Eva told her, tapping three fingers and then moving her hand so that she cupped one palm. Emily heard how the sound changed. 'You try now.'

For almost an hour Emily stayed there, standing in front of a mirror, seeing for herself just how little sense of rhythm she had, but the time flew by.

'Come again tomorrow at this time,' Eva said.

'I don't want to take up your lunch break…'

'You say you have only five weeks here!' Eva pointed out. 'We can do some footwork—you can borrow some shoes, and if you enjoy it then maybe you can get your own, but speak to me first. And Emily!' she called as she left. 'Think about the group workshops. If you want to cram some more lessons in it's a good way to do so, and they are always fun.'

Fun, Emily thought as she dashed back to work. Fun was something that had been missing for far too long from her life.

Yet here in Jerez she was starting to discover it.

She was going out, doing new things, kissing new guys… Well, just the one! But she was finally doing all the things she never had.

After a lifetime of attempting to please people, she was finally taking the time to work out what pleased *her*. It was liberating.

'Alejandro is looking for you,' said Andrés, one of the IT workers, when she returned to the office.

'Good for him,' Emily said, perhaps a little cheekily, but Andrés's English didn't quite stretch to sarcasm, and he gave her a smile and went back to his screen.

'Good for me?' a deep voice said, and Emily swung around.

He looked stunning, with no traces of last night's excesses evident.

'Why is spending the last hour trying to get you on-line for a meeting with Sebastián good for me?'

'I meant…' As Emily took a seat and took a breath, she was a little stunned by her own cheek, and realised she'd come back from her first dance class on a little bit of a high. 'It means…'

'I know exactly what it means, Emily.'

His gorgeous eyes were a little narrowed, as if he was trying to work out the slight change in her, the subtle shift. She knew her outfit was the usual mix of muted shades and practical lines. Her hair was tied up high on her head and was its usual chaotic self. She wore no make-up, but that was usual.

And yet Emily felt a certain defiance as she met his eyes and smiled. 'I'm sorry, Alejandro, I wasn't aware we'd scheduled a meeting.'

'We hadn't,' he conceded. 'That is why I tried to call you.'

She reached into her bag and pulled out her work phone. Sure enough, there were a couple of missed calls from him. It would seem she'd been too busy dancing and discovering *palmas* to hear her phone.

'So you did.' She dropped her bag back in her phone. 'Well, I'm back from lunch now.'

'Excellent,' he said tartly. 'Then can we please get on?'

'Of course.' Emily moved to stand. 'Should I come up to your office?'

'It's an online meeting, Emily. We hardly need to be seated together. There should be an invitation in your inbox.'

Indeed there was.

Emily put on her headphones and logged in, and for a sliver of time she thought the haughty face looking back at her was Alejandro, but quickly she realised it was Sebastián.

'Buenas días,' Emily said.

'Good afternoon,' he responded.

Manhattan was stretched out behind him, but neither of these brothers needed a stunning backdrop, Emily thought, as Alejandro appeared. They might be in the same building, but the view behind Alejandro was like a postcard shot of Jerez. She could see ancient buildings and church spires…the vista from his office was simply to die for.

'Finally,' said Alejandro, by way of greeting. 'Okay, Emily's been here for—'

'Just over a week,' Emily answered for him.

'I just wanted to touch base,' Sebastián said. 'See if you have everything you need and if there are any questions.'

'I have a few.' Emily nodded. 'I'm very keen to meet with Carmen. I'd like to mention her love of the dancing horses and perhaps get some photos of her.'

'That can easily be arranged.' Sebastián nodded. 'Alejandro, have you spoken to Carmen about the new website?'

'Probably not…' Alejandro shrugged. 'I'll give her a call.'

It was at that moment when Emily realised that what was a huge venture for her was just a blip on the radar for the Romeros. They simply wanted it done—their product showcased with a new and refreshing take on things. Certainly they weren't waking up, as she was, to be gripped by a city that was so vibrant it literally danced before your eyes. Nor were they falling asleep wondering how to best capture the image of endless vines and the way they laced across the rolling hills.

That was her job. And, if she wanted to do it well then there were some questions she needed to ask, no matter how awkward they might be.

'I've got a couple of questions about the label, and also your father's biography.'

'You have explained the complexities to Emily?' Sebastián asked his brother.

'Not fully.'

They spoke in Spanish amongst themselves for a couple of minutes, and Emily started to understand that her questions were about the things the brothers were having trouble agreeing on themselves.

They didn't discuss it deeply, but it was clear to her that many an argument had taken place on this very subject.

'Okay…' Sebastián finally addressed Emily. 'For some time we've been considering changing our label. We're working with an artist to produce a watercolour. She's using the same colour themes as the original image, so when we change—'

'*If* we change,' Alejandro interjected.

Emily looked from brother to brother and could almost feel the simmering tension between them.

Sebastián was the oldest, and perhaps thought he wielded more power, but Alejandro, seemingly more laid-back, used his strength quietly. Both were forces to be reckoned with.

Emily sat still and, possibly because she was in Spain, thought of bulls and the old saying about two bulls in one paddock.

Both these men were powerful, both natural leaders, and in this case it would seem they had opposing views.

'At this stage we would really prefer that you focus on the product,' Sebastián said.

'Maria de Luca is *on* the product, though,' Emily attempted, looking from brother to brother. Both faces were determinedly impassive, but she knew Alejandro better and could see that his full lips were pinched tight. 'I don't need to go into detail, or anything, but,' she said, very simply, 'would it help if I discussed this with your father? Find out what *he* wants—?'

'What would help,' Sebastián cut in, 'is for you to work to the brief you've been given.'

'Whoa!' Alejandro said, when usually he would not have done.

But watching his brother dismiss Emily's concerns had provoked him—angered him, even. He did not usually allow anyone to get under his skin, particularly when it was a member of his family—*especially* when it was a member of his family—but he knew how hard it would have been for Emily to ask the question she just had.

'Emily is correct,' Alejandro said. 'This needs to be addressed—preferably before the website goes live. And José would like Maria to be mentioned.'

'Thankfully,' Sebastián put in, 'it is not his decision.'

'No,' Alejandro said. 'It is mine.' He looked at the screen. 'Could you excuse us, please, Emily?'

'Of course.'

'I hope to answer your questions soon.'

They both waited until she was gone.

'We don't discuss internal matters with outsiders,' Sebastián clipped.

'Which is why I asked her to leave,' Alejandro said. 'José wants Maria to stay on the label and for her to be mentioned in his bio.'

'He didn't a few weeks ago—he wanted every trace of her gone!'

'He didn't know he was ill then,' Alejandro responded. 'And it has become my decision—because you and Carmen want her erased, while our father wants her to remain.'

'And what do *you* want?' Sebastián glared at his brother. 'To defend her as you did when we were children? To speak nicely about a woman who walked out on her husband and three children so she could pursue her *art*?'

'Flamenco is an art,' Alejandro said.

He had once loved it, but in more recent years, as he'd realised the damage it had caused to his family, that love had become twisted into first resentment and later indifference.

Watching Eva the other night had brought back some of his love for the art. Seeing Emily, a shy woman who had been ready to leave, remain seated, held utterly spellbound, had awoken some of his own dormant thrill for the ancient art.

It was in his blood, after all.

And it wasn't flamenco that had caused their agony.

It was Maria de Luca, the ice queen herself, who had seen to that.

'Why?' Sebastián asked his brother. 'Why would you support her? Surely we need to move on from her? She had no trouble moving on from us.'

'It's nothing to do with defending her,' Alejandro said. 'It is about our father and respecting his wishes.'

'They change week by week, month by month…'

'I'm aware of that,' Alejandro said, 'and that is why I'm refusing to be rushed into a decision. However, I do need to let Emily know what to do for the website.'

'She can wait,' Sebastián said dismissively. 'Now, while I have you, I spoke to José this morning. He suggests a May wedding…'

'Felicidades!' Alejandro responded, giving his congratulations.

'What?'

'I didn't realise you were even engaged.'

'I'm talking about *your* wedding.'

'Then don't,' Alejandro said—and exited the meeting.

He headed down to the offices and knocked on the door of IT while at the same time walking in.

'Hey,' he said to Andrés, and then walked over to Emily, who was working away at her desk.

'Sorry about that…' he said.

'About what?' She looked up. 'Alejandro, I knew going into that meeting that I'd be raising a difficult topic.'

He perched on the edge of her desk, right beside where she sat, and looked at her rather than the work she was doing.

She tried not to notice.

There was nothing *to* notice, of course.

Everyone else simply carried on working, presumably more used to his presence than she. Yet she could smell that gorgeous cologne…and was rather too aware of his thighs just inches from her hands. More than that, she knew she was blushing and awkward now. She'd arrived back from her first flamenco lesson so exhilarated and bold, but her newfound confidence had soon faded.

'Emily?'

There was a note to his voice that had her stomach folding in on itself, but his rejection still stung, and so she carried on typing as she gave a curt, 'Yes?'

'Can you stop?'

He put his hand over hers and removed it from the keyboard. She refused to acknowledge the effect his touch had, just looked up and somehow managed to meet his eyes.

'Sorry.' She put her hands in her lap and gave him her full attention. 'What did you want to discuss?'

'I can't give you an answer to your question.'

'That's fine,' Emily responded. 'I'll do two versions dealing with the label and your father's bio.'

'That would be best.'

'One more thing,' she said as he moved to go. 'Is there a photo of all five of you? Only I've been through the archives—'

'There's no photo of the five of us.'

'I thought there might be one at the family home. I'm happy to look myself if you just point me in the right direction.'

'There are no photos of the five of us. Maria put on a bit of weight when she was pregnant with Carmen and didn't want to be photographed until she'd recovered her figure.'

'Oh…' Emily said, trying to pretend that what he'd said was completely fine instead of entirely messed up. 'It was just an idea.'

'I would leave that one well alone, too. There really aren't many happy family photos… Maria always liked to be centre stage.'

'Good to know,' she said, and then thought of earlier, when she'd said, *Good for him*, with that sarcastic edge. 'I wasn't being facetious that time. I really do mean it's good to know…'

And it was good to know a little more about him… although of course that wasn't what she was trying to convey.

'I might have started planning a family page or something like that…'

'Well, I've saved you some time.'

'You have.'

'So, you *were* being facetious before?'

'A bit…' she admitted, and watched the way his face was changed by the ghost of a smile.

Aside from the fact that he was incredibly beautiful, there was something about him that moved her. She could see the tension around his eyes and mouth dissolving, just with that small shift of his sensual lips.

They were in an office, with others present, and nothing untoward had happened at all, because Andrés came over, and chatted with Alejandro about cyber land for a moment, and how the sherry was performing on some blockchain.

It was all gobbledegook to Emily, and yet she wished—how she wished—that they would carry on talking for ages, simply because it was so nice to have him here.

'Right,' Alejandro said, as Andrés headed back to his desk. 'I'll let you get on. Two versions...'

'Yes.'

He nodded, and looked at her with brown eyes that seemed to want to say something else...eyes that were dangerous to her self-control.

Eyes that were so dangerous that as she came home from work Emily didn't fully close the front door...

He might see it was open and knock, she thought, knowing she was being pathetic, but somehow letting her desperation override her.

She attempted to be casual and put on the television—some Spanish soap opera, all glittering eyes and jewels, and people so beautiful she felt pale and unsophisticated in comparison.

She poured a glass of wine and then tried to coax the last of her hair serum from the container and do what she could with her wild curls.

Oh, hi... she'd say casually when he knocked and came in, as he had today at the office.

She'd been so sure there was more he'd have said if there hadn't been others around. There was so much still unsaid and undone.

She heard the main gates buzz, and then the sound of his footsteps on the mosaic steps. She held her breath as he climbed the stairs, then halted.

She took a sip of wine but didn't swallow it. Instead her face crumpled as she heard his gates open. It was rather clear that Alejandro Romero had walked right on by and would not be accepting her unvoiced offer to drop in.

Perhaps she should go over there?

What the hell…?

Emily stood up and told herself to have some pride, reminding herself of the talking-to she'd given herself just that morning—sitting watching the sunrise on the very spot where he'd rejected her, telling herself it was time to move on.

She turned off the television angrily—not that the television noticed. And then she picked up her key and before she could talk herself out of it locked the door behind her and determinedly took the stairs.

'Emily!' Eva greeted her warmly. 'You decided to join us.'

'I did.'

Thank heaven for group classes.

She'd been seconds from disaster.

She stood in front of the mirror and picked up the edge of a borrowed shawl, and knew that night she'd been seconds away from making a complete fool of herself and going to him.

'*Quinta!*' Eva said, clapping her hands to gain their attention, and then she raised her hands gracefully in the air. 'Fifth position, Emily. Concentrate.'

Emily loved the group workshop, even if she was dreadful at it—she attended daily when her schedule allowed, and certainly nightly when the Alejandro urge hit.

She borrowed from Eva's selection of flamenco shoes, though rather guiltily she intended to splurge and buy some expensive professional ones, even if they would only serve as a souvenir of her time here. On Saturday she'd been to a flea market at Mercadillo José

Ignacio, a pleasant walk from the city centre, and had bought a practice skirt and top. She took these lessons seriously, and even had her own piece of wood to practise on at home.

A heel strike was a *tacón*.

Using the sole of her foot, *planton*.

And *golpe* meant she struck the floor with the whole of her foot.

Eva was a hard taskmaster.

'Come on, Emily, we only have four more weeks. You are like a tree that refuses to bend.'

She always singled Emily out but, given the limited time span, Emily tried to accept the criticism rather than burst into tears and run, as she sometimes felt like doing.

'Be provocative, Emily,' Eva told her now, in the one-to-one class she'd squeezed into her day.

What was the point of being provocative? Emily thought. She'd practically thrown herself at him.

'Emily, *move*,' Eva urged.

'I am,' Emily said, trying to inject some sass into her hips. But Eva was right. She was like a lump of wood that refused to bend to any wind.

Oh, but she tried.

'Tonight, *jaleo*…' Eva said, as Emily slipped off her practice skirt, changed her shoes and took a gulp of water at the end of her class.

'What's that?'

'Hellraising!' Eva smiled. 'Dress up and I shall see you here at eight.'

'If I finish work in time.'

She often didn't, Emily thought, as she made her way back from her midday flamenco class to work, with a tiny detour to the Plaza Santiago to buy a gorgeous handbag she had seen for Anna.

It was the softest leather, and although Emily would never spend that much on a bag for herself, it was perfect for a busy single mum who juggled work and childcare.

As well as that, there wasn't going to be much more time for lingering in the shops. She was pulling twelve-hour days at work, and often continued until late at night. Two weeks were already gone and she still hadn't got the shots she wanted—nor had she spoken with Carmen and seen the horses.

Everyone in the office looked at her sideways when she did dash off, but no one ever asked where she was going—and anyway, she had her answer ready: she was learning more about the local culture.

Oh, and Emily loved it.

As she walked through Plaza de Santiago she checked her phone. But, no, work hadn't called. There was just a missed call from Anna, so she quickly buzzed her back.

'How is it?' asked Anna.

'Incredible,' Emily admitted, taking a second to pause and take in the fountain, the cafés and churches, still unable to believe she was actually here. 'I'm going to get Willow a flamenco dress.'

'Please don't!' Anna said.

'Seriously, they're gorgeous. How is she doing?'

'Another ear infection…' Anna sighed. 'Tell me what you're up to. She loves hearing about it.'

'Well, I still haven't seen the dancing horses, but tell her I'm working on it. Honestly, Anna, there's so much to see and take in, but I'm working on a few ideas and starting to get a feel for it for now. Alejandro said not to rush.'

'Alejandro?'

'He's one of the brothers.'

Emily's face was on fire. She wanted to confide in her friend, but just didn't know what she could possibly say. Alejandro's reaction to her virginity hadn't exactly been inspiring. And so, instead of talking about anything deeply personal she chatted about her dance classes and how she was going to do an online course with Eva when she returned home.

'Flamenco?' Anna checked, as if her rather staid and sensible friend had gone completely mad.

'It is *life*!' Emily said dramatically, as the Jerez people did, and was laughing as she ended the call.

And then she looked up at the church and frowned when she saw the spire.

Oh, my goodness!

Was that a nest?

'Hey...'

It was Alejandro, looking amazing in a charcoal-grey suit and eating a bag of potato crisps. But for once she was able to play it cool, so focussed on the church spire was she.

She turned, but only briefly. Her focus was on the church, or rather the spire above it, and she was grateful for the intriguing distraction. 'Is that a nest?'

'For sure.' He looked up too. 'It's a stork's nest.'

'It's huge!'

'They need to be.'

'Look!' she squealed as a face popped up. 'There's one in there. Oh, I wish I'd brought my camera.'

'They're everywhere.' He smiled. 'In most church

spires. They come from Africa across the Strait of Gibraltar. It means spring is here…'

Alejandro looked for a moment at Emily rather than up at the spire. She was squinting into the bright midday sun, and looking rushed and breathless, yet still she'd stopped to admire the nest.

'He's waiting for his mate, getting the nest ready.'

'They're monogamous, aren't they?'

'No.' Alejandro was quick to break any fantasy she held. 'That's just a myth.'

'Surely not? I'm sure I read that they mate for life.'

'Then you read wrong—or it was a fairy tale.' He thought for a moment. 'I believe they stay faithful while their mate is alive…'

'Oh…'

'They're good while it lasts,' Alejandro said, and poured some of his crisps on his palm.

He offered her one, but Emily declined and watched him as he chose the biggest one for himself.

'Why are you out here eating crisps?' she asked.

'I love them. But if I call down to the kitchen for crisps they put them in a dish and all the salt falls off.'

'What are you talking about…the salt falls off?'

'They don't taste as good.' He looked back up at the nest. 'Also, these storks you think are so cute kill the weakest of their chicks.'

'No!' She put her hands over her ears. 'That's horrible.' Though he had made her laugh. 'Why would you tell me that?'

'To see you cringe.' He smiled, and then looked

back up at the nest. 'Though I stand corrected…both are there.'

'Which one's the female?'

'I have no clue,' he admitted. 'How are you doing?'

'Well—I hope. The website's coming on, and everyone's being really helpful.'

'I meant how are *you* doing?'

'Fine!' She bristled, wishing she could say it with more conviction…wishing her hurt wasn't so raw and visible.

Gordon's breaking up with her had hurt way less than Alejandro's rejection.

His eyes moved to her latest purchase. 'That's a nice bag.'

'It's not for me,' Emily said quickly, embarrassed by the extravagance of her purchase. 'I bought it for my friend.'

'Well, it would suit you.' He looked at her face and she knew she was blushing. 'You deserve nice things.'

'I have nice things,' Emily said. 'Actually, I've seen a tripod…' He stared back at her with unblinking velvet-brown eyes. 'It's so light, and it folds up to practically nothing.'

He frowned—not a frown as such, but the skin around his eyes crinkled a little.

'That's for business,' he said. 'I meant something nice for *you*.'

'I love my work.'

'It's no longer a hobby, though,' he pointed out, his slight frown remaining and his eyes steadfastly upon her, as if assessing her reaction as he spoke. 'Eva says you're enjoying the flamenco classes?'

'She told you I've been taking them?'

'Yes, she said you are very…' He thought for a moment. 'English.'

'What does that mean?'

'Very formal, and not brilliant at being expressive.'

She gaped, feeling appalled. 'She's not allowed to tell you that!'

'Hey, I didn't know there was a flamenco code of confidentiality.' He seemed to be laughing at her embarrassment. 'Anyway, I've heard you practising.'

'You can hear me? I thought those walls were thick enough to block any noise out.'

'They are…' He frowned again, probably at her embarrassment. 'I just hear when I pass your door.'

'So you know how out of time I am?'

'Don't be too hard on yourself.'

'I know I'm not going to master it in six weeks— well, four weeks now. We've got *jaleo* tonight…'

'Ole!'

'I'm dreading it,' she admitted. 'I just can't…'

'What?'

'I don't know… I just feel so awkward.' She told her one of Eva's suggestions. 'Eva says I'm to wear red lipstick for my next class.'

'Why?' He frowned again.

'She thinks it might make me smile more.'

'But you're always smiling,' he said. 'You have a beautiful smile.'

'I don't…' She shook her head, because she knew she wasn't being self-effacing. 'Eva's right. I don't readily smile.'

She stopped then. Her explanation was causing more questions as his words started to sink in. All her life she'd been told to smile more, that she was too serious—she'd even joked with Willow that she'd been born with a serious face. Yet with Alejandro she smiled easily. It was as if he'd freed her lips—not just to smile but to speak more easily.

'I think you see a slightly more smiley version of me than everybody else,' she told him.

'Do I?'

She nodded. 'I'd better get some lipstick, I guess.'

Alejandro said nothing. In truth, he was a little shaken by what she had just said.

Just a couple of days ago Eva had thanked him for recommending Señorita Seria to come and see her.

'Who?' Alejandro had asked.

'The English girl…we call her Señorita Seria…'

Miss Serious.

And he remembered how, after one of their online meetings, when Emily had gone, Sebastián had rolled his eyes and spoken about their sullen new website designer…

Sullen? Alejandro would never have described her as such.

If she went missing and he was the last person to see her, he'd tell the police about her blue eyes and bright smile. How her untamed curls had a life of their own, and how she argued over storks in a nest, how she made him laugh and smile…

It almost killed Alejandro to hear her practising.

Last night, as he'd made his way up the stairs, he'd heard her. He'd stood there for a moment, trying not to picture her, tempted to knock, but instead he'd made his way through the gates to the safe silence of heavy brick walls.

Here he was, insisting she'd be better off without him, when it would seem that she neither wanted nor needed his care or concern.

He was coming around to the idea that maybe she *could* take the part-time nature of his affection....

Emily fascinated him. She was gentle and she was shy, and yet there was a strength to her he admired immensely. She had no family—a concept he could barely grasp—and she made her own way...taking dance lessons in a foreign country, kissing him amongst the vines, fighting to be brave...

He tried to catch her eyes, but she was glancing at the time.

'I'd better get back,' she said. 'If I'm to have any hope of making it to *jaleo* tonight.'

'Have fun,' Alejandro said. 'You should enjoy your time here.'

'I intend to,' Emily said, and with a brief wave and smile she headed back towards the bodega, wishing any brief conversation with Alejandro didn't affect her so. And wishing that seeing the storks' nest, or her dance class, or even *jaleo* tonight might prove to be the highlight of her day, rather than her few minutes alone with him.

Don't worry, Alejandro, she thought to herself, *I shall enjoy my time here.*

She was determined to.

A little *too* determined, perhaps.

CHAPTER EIGHT

'Okay!' Eva clapped her hands and forced the chattering to stop. 'Tonight we are going to go over to the courtyard at Bodega Romero…'

'Romero?' Emily frowned. 'But I work there.'

She had followed Eva's instructions and indeed dressed up for tonight. She was wearing the pink practice skirt with violet flowers that she had bought at the thrift market, and had added the violet top that had come with it. She'd never intended to wear it—the low-cut top showed way too much cleavage—but she was really trying to give the classes her all. She was also wearing a borrowed pair of red flamenco shoes, and to top things off had tied a big silk rose in her hair.

Though she hadn't gone out and bought the recommended red lipstick, Emily had thought she was well and truly ready for hellraising—but only in the safety of Eva's studio!

'I thought tonight was *jaleo*?'

'It is.' Eva nodded. 'The restaurant is closed on a Monday, so we can make noise there…'

Emily inwardly groaned. There was no way she was going to get up on stage in front of her colleagues—especially if one of them happened to be Alejandro.

'Is *jaleo* always held at Romero?' Emily asked.

'Pretty much.' Eva nodded.

Bastard, Emily thought. He'd known all along. He could have at least warned her. Well, there was no way she was getting up on that stage.

Eva must have seen her gritting her jaw. 'Just sit and watch if you are too timid to join in, Emily,' she said. 'Now, can you please carry the shawls? Stella, can you bring the castanets?'

Thankfully, having trooped through Plaza de Santiago and arrived at the bodega, she saw no sign of Alejandro, but even so there was no way she was joining in.

She sat at the courtyard bar as the rest of the class took to the stage. People were drinking, idly watching the assembled dancers. Emily simply didn't know how to get up and just dance as the others did.

There was a lot of stamping of male feet as the dancers took to the stage, and Emily baulked at even the thought of the final hurdle. Or rather the stairs to the stage.

'Maybe later,' she mumbled to herself.

'Gracias,' she said to the barman, who knew her by now, of course, and smiled when she ordered a diet cola.

'Why aren't you dancing?' he asked.

'Soon!' Emily said, and then offered by way of explanation, 'I've only just finished work.'

'Hola.'

She heard a male voice, but knew without turning her head that it wasn't Alejandro.

'You're not dancing?' the man asked.

'No.' Emily flashed a polite smile. 'Perhaps later.'

'Would you like another drink?'

'No, thank you,' Emily said.

Not that it stopped him from trying to make conversation.

His name was Fernando and, if she was being completely honest, a couple of weeks ago she'd have been both thrilled and embarrassed to be chatted up by this man. Her rock-bottom ego would have glowed as red as her cheeks at Fernando's skilled flirting.

Now, though, she felt numb.

Just utterly numb as he moved his stool a little closer and told her how gorgeous her outfit was.

'I love to see a woman dressed in bright colours…'

Emily looked down at her hastily put-together outfit. It was just so not her—and neither was sitting on a bar stool next to a stranger.

It had felt so easy when she'd sat in the *taberna* with Alejandro. So simple to make her way to his table and simply enjoy the night.

Now all she felt was a little less numb and possibly a little bit sad…

And then the man she really wanted to flirt with unexpectedly walked in, and her ego glowed a little at the thought that she wasn't sitting alone at the bar.

Alejandro was carrying a large, flat white box under his arm and walking briskly towards his residence, not wanting to get waylaid in conversation. But then, out of the corner of his eye, he saw blonde curls and glanced over. His reaction was purely mental, but it felt so physical it was like a punch low in the guts as he saw Emily's pretty face turn to her admirer.

What the hell…?

It was none of his business, though he'd been about to make it so.

He tossed the box down on to a table and gestured to the bar staff for a drink.

They were startled into attention, unused to the boss taking an aperitif in the courtyard, particularly during a dance lesson. Usually he'd be punching out two headache tablets from a blister pack on his way past, rather than taking a seat.

Not tonight.

'Gracias,' he said to the barman as his drink was placed down, but though he was polite his eyes never left Emily and her new *friend*.

She was leaning forward to catch whatever it was he'd just said, and Señorita Seria seemed to have discovered how to laugh, because she kept throwing her head back and laughing, when Alejandro knew that Fernando wasn't in the least funny.

Now she was swirling her straw in her glass, just blatantly flirting...

He could take it no more and walked over.

'Emily?' She felt Alejandro tap her shoulder. 'Do you have a minute?'

'I'm actually at a dance class.'

She could see his dark eyes glinting and knew this was not about business.

'Well, you're not exactly dancing,' Alejandro said tartly. 'It will just take a few moments of your precious time.'

She turned to look at him, about to point out that it was after-hours, but one glance at his black expression had her biting her lip.

'Excuse me a moment,' she said to the very vain Fernando, who was looking into the bar mirror and smoothing his hair as she slid down from her stool.

She went to follow Alejandro to his table, but instead of taking his seat he picked up a box and gestured towards the gates to his residence.

'In private.'

He smiled a black mirthless smile, and she watched his tense fingers type in the code, but once the gates had closed behind him all attempts at niceties subsided.

'What the hell are you doing?' he demanded.

'I don't know what you're talking about.'

'Don't give me that.' He was not mincing his words. 'You and Fernando were practically on top of each other.'

'We were talking,' Emily said. 'It's nice to talk with someone who's actually attracted to me.'

'Fernando's a player.'

'Well, that's not your concern—you've made that very clear.'

'Are you so determined to lose your virginity?' He took her arm, as if trying to shake some sense into her, as direct and as blunt as ever. 'Just for the sake of it?'

'Go to hell!'

He did not go to hell, though.

As she wrenched open the gates to return to the courtyard he followed her out. And when she took her seat back at the bar he took his own at the table.

Arrogant idiot, Emily thought.

'What did he want?' Fernando asked.

'Just work stuff.'

'Another drink?' offered Fernando.

'No, thank you.'

'A dance then…?' he said, and put his hand over hers.

Emily knew she was playing a dangerous game. She didn't want Fernando at all.

'No, thank you.' Emily gave him a tight smile and got down from the stool a little awkwardly.

God, she felt pathetic. She turned, ready to meet Alejandro's glare, but saw that he had got bored with her stupid game and gone.

'Emily…'

Eva, too, was possibly trying to save her from Fernando, and was calling her to join the dancers on the stage. But instead she turned to speak with her.

'I think I'm going to call it a night.'

'Perdón?'

'I'm going to go up.'

'Oh,' Eva said, and did not try to dissuade her, but got back to the rest of the class.

Emily wanted to hide, completely embarrassed by her own actions. She was so out of her depth when it came to men, or relationships.

A few tears spilled down her cheeks as she hurriedly made her way towards her apartment. She went to open up her front door, and then turned and looked at the gate behind her—the entrance to Alejandro's residence—and knew he deserved an apology.

But did she dare?

Oh, she wasn't going to his door out of temptation, or to throw herself at him—thankfully she had got over that…

Really, it didn't take a mirror to tell her she wasn't looking her best, with her face red from crying and her mismatched outfit and the silk flower in her hair.

She just wanted to thank him for looking out for her and to say sorry…

* * *

Alejandro had poured himself a drink and was fighting with himself not to go back down to the courtyard and wrench Emily away from that creep, and at the same time telling himself it was not his place to do so.

As Emily had just pointed out, she was not his concern.

Then he heard the tentative knock on his door and opened it. And what he saw further exacerbated the recent thaw of his usually cold and emotionless heart. Emily was shaking in her attempt to suppress tears… so much so, the silk rose was almost falling out of her hair. Her face was flushed and she couldn't look at him.

It was he who spoke first. 'Emily, I apologise.'

'For what?'

'I overreacted. You have every right to…' He rolled his hand, but couldn't bring himself to say *flirt with whoever you want* without sounding bitter. 'But Fernando's a player, Emily.'

'Alejandro, I was just… I was trying to make you jealous.'

'That's not very sensible,' he said gently.

'I know.'

And he could have lectured her, but who the hell was he to scold her?

'It worked.'

She looked up, embarrassed, but so grateful that rather than being scathing he was being nice. With Alejandro she had always been honest, and she was being honest now.

'But don't do that again,' he warned. 'It might not end so well next time.'

'I know.' She took a breath. 'I am sorry.'

'Forget it,' he said.

'Thank you for warning me,' she said.

And she really wasn't here for anything more than that, so, taking her wounded pride, Emily turned from his door.

'Hey, Emily?'

'What?' She looked back over her shoulder.

'Why don't you come in and flirt with me?'

Still she didn't turn around, and she remained honest. 'Because you don't want me, and it hurts too much.'

'Stop it!' he said. 'You know that's not true.'

He left the door open and went inside, entirely giving Emily the option whether to leave or go in.

She stepped inside, not into a hallway, but into a dark, sensual space.

His residence was stunning.

Male, sexy, vast…

And unlike in her little apartment there were no sounds coming up from the street or the courtyard.

The walls were white, hung with ancient hangings and a few musical instruments, as well as a lot of art. Random sculptures were dotted about the place. The place was like a very stylish and muted Aladdin's cave—or rather a grown-up Aladdin's cave. Because rather than garish jewels, everywhere she looked there was a subtle treasure…a chest, a piece of art…a guitar…

The room also contained a pair of low leather couches and she perched on the edge of one as he offered her a drink.

'A gin and tonic,' Emily said, as his hand hovered over the black Romero sherry bottle.

'I'd have to call down to the bar for that.'

'A brandy, then,' Emily said. 'Or cognac.'

He poured her a generous measure of cognac and she took it silently and stared at it for a very long time, not really knowing what to say. Then she plucked at the awful skirt that had felt so right for fun in the studio, but was not her outfit of choice when sitting in the home of this very sophisticated man.

Then he spoke.

'You make me smile, too,' he said suddenly.

Emily looked up from the depths of her gloom, wondering if she'd missed something he said.

Possibly he saw her confusion.

'I was thinking about it after we met at lunchtime. I didn't get it that Eva said you needed help to smile, or...' He took a breath. 'Emily, from the day I met you, you've always smiled.'

'I'm actually quite serious,' Emily said. 'When I'm not frantically on the pull with Fernando...'

'See?' Alejandro said.

And she looked up and saw that he smiled. It had never occurred to her that it might be rare for him too.

'I want you to have an amazing time while you're here, and I'd love to spend time with you, but you have to understand I am not into relationships. Believe me, if you want more than bed then I am not your man.'

'You are, though...' She shivered. That had come out sounding too needy. 'I mean, I want bed,' she admitted. 'With you.'

'I don't want tears at the end,' Alejandro said. 'I told you...ending things doesn't have to be complicated.'

'I know. I've just got this...' Still she was able to be truthful. 'I didn't know how a kiss should be until I kissed you. I have a past. I've seemingly lived with someone…been engaged. And yet I feel like I've got a millstone around my neck…'

'A millstone?'

'A weight on my shoulders,' she said, trying to explain something so intensely personal to the man with those dark, knowing eyes. He made her articulate things… 'I don't want to be a virgin. It makes me seem…' She looked at him. 'It put *you* off.'

'No,' he said. 'It caused me to hesitate.'

'Please don't lie when I'm being so honest.'

'Okay,' he said, and gave her the truth. 'It did put me off. I was already a little hesitant, given we're working together, and with all that's going on in my private life…'

'Your fiancée?'

'We were never formally engaged—but, yes. I didn't want to stir gossip. I wanted you, though. And then you told me that you'd never slept with anyone and it felt too much. I thought that if you'd waited this long then you should be very sure—'

'Do you know what?' she interrupted, and looked right at him. 'I like you.'

It was the bravest she had ever been. Braver than flying to Jerez or walking into a flamenco studio. Braver than coming to his door to admit she'd been foolish. Just brave.

'I have an awful lot of hang-ups, and sometimes I forget them when I'm with you. Maybe I like the fact that we can go nowhere. That I can talk openly to you.'

Even with her face on fire, even cringing with embarrassment, Emily could not think of anyone else she could have had this conversation with.

'I don't want it to be a big deal—except it is. I don't

want to be a virgin and have some guy telling me that if I've waited this long then I ought to be "very sure…" as if I don't know my own mind.'

'Hey…' He winced at his own choice of words. 'I just said that—'

'Well, don't say it again. Because I am sure. I want you—physically, at least. It doesn't mean I'm going to fall in love with you. I know you're not interested in long-term. I just want to make love with someone I want.'

'Fine,' Alejandro said. 'I won't warn you again. I've already told you I'm a bastard.'

'I want to be like the storks,' Emily said.

'God, no.' He shook his head. 'I looked it up. They are monogamous for the life of their mate…'

'I meant,' Emily said, 'I don't want there to be anyone else for as long as we last.'

'That's my rule too.'

Finally some common ground.

'And I have another rule,' Alejandro said. 'We have to be discreet.'

'What do you mean?'

'I don't want anyone finding out about us.'

Her eyes narrowed. She was not quite sure as to his reason.

'Emily, I don't bring my entire life to work.'

'You *have* broken things off with Mariana?' she checked.

'Yes. I'd just reminded her that we were over on the night we met,' he told her, and then asked a question of his own. 'If you know I'm that much of a player, what are you doing here?'

Emily gave a tight shrug.

She wasn't feeling quite so bold now. She'd liked it better out in the vineyards, when it had just happened so easily. Now she felt a little as if she were in the doctor's waiting room, and that at any moment she'd be called in.

God, she was so jumpy, but trying not to show it, Emily thought, as he came and took a seat on the sofa beside her.

'Why didn't you dance tonight?' he asked. 'Aside from…'

He didn't want to say Fernando's name, Emily realised.

'How come you didn't get up on the stage?'

'Because I would have looked ridiculous.'

'Why? You were looking forward to *jaleo*.'

'Yes. When I thought it was going to be held in the studio.' She shook her head. 'I'm really not very good at dancing. Eva says I'm like a tree that won't bend.'

'Maybe this will help… I've got you a present.'

'What?' She frowned. 'Why?'

'Like I said, I was thinking about you today.'

She realised the white box he had been carrying was actually for her.

'Open it,' he said.

She peeled open the edge and then pulled back handfuls of tissue paper. Atop some layers of red fabric was a pair of black leather flamenco shoes. Turning them over, she saw that the nails were already banged in. These were serious shoes…more beautiful than she would have ever chosen for herself.

'Alejandro, they're for a professional.'

'They make an amazing noise.'

'But how did you know my size?'

'Eva can be discreet when required.'

'You told her!'

'I said I wanted to get you some shoes and asked which ones you practised in.' He shrugged. 'I said you were trying to find out more about flamenco for the website.'

'Do you think she believed you?'

'I don't know about that. I just know she would never say anything.'

She could not quite contemplate that Alejandro had left her looking at the church spire and gone to Eva, and then gone shopping with her in mind.

'Why would you do this?' she asked.

'Why not?' He sounded bemused. 'I wanted to get you something nice. You deserve it. Maybe I wanted to treat the strongest woman I know.'

'Please…' She rolled her eyes. 'Don't go too over the top.'

'But you are. I cannot imagine living my life without family. Yet you do.'

'Alejandro, for years I hid behind a man who didn't want me.'

'Yet here you are, taking dance classes in a foreign country…starting your own business. Emily, I thought my mother was strong, but she always had her parents behind her, or my father, or a lover.'

She'd never been called strong before. It was almost laughable, and yet his eyes were serious.

She looked at the box of gifts. There was also a gold tube of lipstick, and beneath the shoes something in a sheer, silky fabric that intrigued her…

'What's this?'

'It's a flamenco dress,' he said. 'Modern flamenco,' he added.

'I've never seen one like this.'

'They are not in most stores,' he said. 'It's not something you'd wear to the studio.'

'Then where?'

She touched the silk as if it were hot coals, sharply pulling her hand back.

'You want to dance? Dance for *me*, then.'

She stared at him.

'Go on.'

'I can't wear this,' she said, holding up the very sheer dress. 'I'll look ridiculous.'

'Why do you say that?' He was impatient. 'You don't need to have a degree in flamenco to wear it... you don't have to reach some high standard. Go and get changed...tonight we make our own *jaleo*.'

'Do you play the guitar?'

'Good God, no.'

He smiled and, standing, took out a vinyl record. As she stood there, the sounds of a guitar and a *cajón* filled the room.

'You can use my bedroom to change.'

He said it so casually...as if her going to his bedroom to get changed was normal.

'Straight down the hall.'

The hall was long, the huge wooden doors at the end were already open, and she clipped towards them, hearing the tinny metal sounds her borrowed shoes were making on the tiles.

The room was softly lit and the low bed was dressed in white. The scent of his cologne hung in the air, and it felt oddly like an unwanted reprieve to be in here without him.

If he really wanted her, wouldn't it be *his* hands undressing her?

She looked at the bed and it terrified her, but then she looked into the mirror and that worried her even more.

She stood there, alone in his bedroom, in front of a full-length mirror, and decided that anything she put on now would surely be an improvement on this.

Her purple practice skirt and plunging top looked as if she'd been raiding the dress-up box at some amateur theatre club. The flower in her hair had fallen down and now hung from one curl. She peeled off her clothes and looked at her underwear, which was by far too sensible for the new dress.

She pulled the dress over her head, absolutely certain that it would never stretch enough and could never fit…yet the liquid silky fabric meshed to her body like a second skin.

The neckline was far too low for her to wear her T-shirt bra beneath it. And her awful knickers did nothing for the clinging fabric.

She slid them off, but the fabric now clung to her bare stomach, so she took down the sleeves and removed her bra.

Then she slid the arms of the dress back on.

She was fully dressed, but her nipples were thick and the fabric so sheer she could see her tummy button. Somehow it clung and yet it smoothed, making her breasts and stomach look shapely. It hugged her bottom and thighs.

Sitting on the edge of the bed, she lifted the skirt as she slid on her shoes and saw that, even though it clung, there was yard after yard of fabric in the dress.

God, it was too sexy by far, Emily thought as, with her new shoes on, she looked in the mirror.

Now she looked as if she'd raided the costume box of some upmarket opera house.

Tonight, Carmen will be played by Emily, she thought, laughing to herself and retying her silk flower.

She turned around and saw that the back of the dress was so low it revealed most of her spine, then she spun back to the mirror.

Her red cheeks looked as if she'd been slapped and they stung in her pale face.

She took out the lipstick and painted her mouth red, and then she walked out.

The shoes sounded fabulous, the metal nails ringing out with each step she took, and there was no chancing of pausing or taking tentative steps because she knew that he'd hear her.

She was one burning blush as she entered his lounge.

His tie and jacket were off and he had changed into boots rather than the shoes he'd had on before.

And he was watching her in a way she had never been looked at in her life.

'Come closer,' he said, and turned on a side light.

She wished he hadn't, because she'd felt a little less exposed in the semi-darkness.

Now shadows fell, and she could see his expression as he looked at her hair and her neck. He stared at her breasts for so long that they ached, and she wanted to touch them. He gazed at her stomach, and she wanted to suck it in, but it was way too late for that.

'You look incredible…'

'Stop.'

'How do you feel?'

'Somewhere between a fraud and amazing.' She was shaking, but with excitement, and the dress was somehow cool on her inflamed skin.

'Lift the hem of the dress.'

'I haven't got any knickers on.'

He laughed, a low sexy laugh, and then corrected her assumption. 'I meant lift it at one side.'

'Oh.'

'I'm not asking you to flash me.'

She started to giggle. To relax just a touch.

She leaned forward and with her right hand lifted the hem of her dress. It unfurled as she held her arm out to one side.

'Higher,' he said, and she held it up high.

The fabric lifted as if with miles to spare. The dress really was incredible. She ached to look down, but remembered her classes and kept her chin up.

'Dance for me, *señorita*.'

He struck the floor with his foot and then clapped— or, as she now knew, gave a *palma*. One, two, three, *palmas* that shot arrows of lust to her stomach. And then he followed that with cupped *palmas* as his foot struck the floor again.

She struck back with her heel. Then her toe, then her sole. Then she gave a *palma* back at him and moved her hips. And then he smiled appreciatively and she *did* know how to dance, it would seem. But perhaps there was no one else in the world she could do this in front of.

Not even Eva.

She moved her hips and walked forward, and then she lifted the dress and swayed with it, and, God, she might not be sexy, but he made her feel it.

He was stamping one foot and that made her move faster. The rolling sound of the guitar and the *cajón* made her feel a little frenzied. It was accompanied by the sound of men singing and cheering, and she could see he was turned on.

He stood up and she danced a little dance around him.

'I feel stup—'

'Shut up and be sexy,' he told her.

And then made her quiet with his mouth; with hot wet kisses as still she moved to the music.

His lithe body barely moved, but each motion, each stamp of his foot or clap of his hand, spun her, so that she continued to dance around him.

His hand slid to her waist and it felt hot through the fabric. They were just dancing bodies, loose but close, and then he caught her in his arms so that her back was to him, and she stood breathless as he kissed her neck.

His mouth was on her flickering pulse, his tongue on her flesh had her pressing into him, and she closed her eyes at the bliss of his lips on her neck and his hand on her breasts.

'Not so wooden...' he said, and turned her as easily as if the floor was revolving beneath her.

He kissed her hard on the mouth, the music still playing, their hips still swaying. Then he removed his belt as his tongue chased hers, and she opened up his shirt with desperate fingers.

His skin, his torso, was so incredible that she had to see it, and she explored his arms, his shoulders, his chest and toned stomach and he made her dizzy with lust.

He had moved the fabric of the dress so that her breasts spilled out, and now they were locked in mutual admiration as they resumed kissing, their naked chests pressed together.

'I thought,' he admitted as he kissed her down on to the couch, 'that I would have to drag you from the bedroom.'

'I told you…' Emily gazed up at him. 'I want you.'

Perhaps her confidence was the new sexy…? Or was it just the absolute desire in her eyes? Because, with Emily, he thought he might have veered from his more practised moves. But hearing her wanton voice, feeling the way she licked at his ear as her hands slid over his torso, Alejandro was in uncharted territory.

But not quite.

He was kissing her breasts, lifting the skirt of her dress, as he recalled they had been here before. Last time they had been in the vineyard, where they'd been just utterly lost to each other.

Now they were warm, and sexed up, and there was nothing to stop them.

'Christ…' he said, lowering his head, licking down her neck and bare chest.

He slid her arms out of the dress so that she was naked from the waist up. And then so practised and skilled were his fingers that he moved the garment down her hips, as if he were unpeeling her, exposing her.

Now all she wore were her shoes…her gorgeous, beautiful new shoes. And as she lifted one foot up to admire them he saw the shining pinkness of her, and held her leg higher and placed it on his shoulder.

Her hand shot out to cover herself but he caught it.

She licked her lips a little nervously, but then bravely lifted the other leg.

'I was going to take you to bed,' he said, stroking her. 'But instead I am on my knees…'

He lowered his head and licked up her thigh. He nipped at the tender skin so that she writhed, and then she stopped fighting as his mouth found her centre.

He was so slow and so thorough and so noisy in his pleasure that she thought she might die. She lay rocked by the waves that swept through her, trying to resist them.

'Go with it,' he told her.

'I can't,' she admitted.

Because no matter how delicious the feeling of his mouth on her body, she could not give in to it while knowing there was more to come.

His erection was huge, and perhaps he saw the trepidation in her eyes, because he knelt up and they touched it together…

'Don't stop,' she begged. 'I never knew…'

'God…' he moaned.

'Please…' she said.

His mouth felt amazing…her only regret was that it was only she who was weak.

'You're so hot…' His naked torso came up to hers. 'We're going to bed. Condoms…?'

'I'm on the pill.'

'Emily,' he warned, 'you don't have unprotected sex with a man you picked up from a *taberna*.'

He was kneeling up…rubbing her breasts and batting her thigh with his erection.

'It's *you*, though…' Her voice sounded breathy and

wanton…she didn't want to move from this heavy bliss.
'You're not dangerous.'

She should have heard the warning in her own words.
But she could not have done this with another man—not
even her fiancé, had he wanted her. With Alejandro it
felt normal to be kissing with reckless passion and to
be desperate for the feel of the other's skin.

She could only have been like this with him, and
they were both too far gone to dwell on anything other
than the other.

The record had stopped and the needle was making little scratching noises. He could hear her ragged breath-
ing as she looked down to where he stroked himself.

She was glistening wet, from desire and his tongue.
The scent of her turned on was heady, and the taste of
her had driven him wild. He could not resist a feel of
her. In truth, he wanted to gauge her pain and her pleasure, but he wasn't all gentleman—he wanted to feel
her too.

'I'm going to so lecture you later,' he said.

But for now…

He eased in a little way and watched her pale thighs
tremble, heard her little moan as he inched in further.

'Please…'

It wasn't the pain Emily was terrified of—more that
he might stop.

'Shh…'

His finger stroked her and then slipped inside, as
if he were toying with that idea, but then he came up
and kissed her.

His kisses were like oxygen, just completely necessary, and it was Emily who turned her head as he nudged in deeper than he had before.

It hurt, and she tried to hold on to her moan.

'Oh, God...' She turned her face away and screwed her eyes closed.

'Emily!'

He called her name and she faced him. With one hand he caressed her face as the other held his thick length. It was the most delicious moment of her life to date.

They were staring at each other as he drove in, making a breathless sound as he tore through the barrier of resistance, and she sobbed—but it was a moan of both pain and desire.

'Oh, Alejandro...' She was clinging to his back, feeling the silky skin and taut muscles beneath, and her eyes closed as she tried to acclimatise to the feel of him inside her.

He started to move, slow thrusts that made tears squeeze from her eyes, and her teeth bit into her lip as she arched at the new sensations. She did not know how to move, but she knew he did not require her expertise—she had none. So she gave in to his.

He took her leg and pushed it back, then did the same with the other, and she cried out as he drove in deeper. It felt as if she were being swallowed, or buried, as if she were being consumed...

'There...' she said, although what 'there' meant she did not know. She knew just that this was everything she wanted.

'Alej...' She had never shortened his name until now, but she was dropping syllables with her every inhibition, pleading with him for more of whatever this magic was.

He was moving deeper, and faster, and she realised just how controlled he was only when he let go a little.

His thrusts were building…he was holding her thighs open and watching them…and then he put his forearms either side of her head and took her fast.

'Ah…'

The last syllables fell away. Emily could not have shouted his name if she'd tried, because her jaw was tense.

She was twisting, but not moving, because his body had her pinned, and she gave in to the pleasure—just succumbed. His sudden shout, the way he stilled and then came deep within her, was a sensation overload, and she cried out again. Not in pain, nor regret, just in the release he gave her.

'It's okay…'

She didn't mind her tears. They seemed normal when her every emotion felt as if it had been leeched from her.

'Hey…' he said, scooping her up and finally taking her to his bed.

It didn't intimidate her now.

CHAPTER NINE

EMILY WAS FALLING in love.

But determinedly not with Alejandro.

She would not allow herself to do that because it wasn't a part of their deal, so instead she told herself that it was the city and its surroundings that so deeply appealed.

She was falling in love with the food and the buzzing atmosphere, the spontaneous singing and dancing that broke out not just in the *peñas*, but as people walked in the street.

And as well as all that there were her dance lessons.

'Alfojar!' Eva would repeatedly tell her. *Relax, loosen...*

And over and over she was told to smile. She was told to be sexy, told to be angry. Eva would pat herself under her own chin and Emily would raise her head higher. Or Eva would draw a swift semi-circle near her own lips and that would tell Emily to smile.

'Chin up!' Eva said. 'And smile. Show how you are feeling. You are happy, yes...?'

'Yes!' she answered instantly.

Two weeks with Alejandro and she was the happiest she had ever been. She felt adored, wanted and, yes…happy.

'Then show it,' Eva said. 'We have just two weeks left.'

Her smile faltered then, but Emily quickly snapped it back, determined to keep to her side of the deal. A holiday romance was what she had wanted. Breaking up didn't have to be complicated, Alejandro had said, and she'd told him with certainty that she could handle a short-term relationship.

'You are confident,' Eva said.

'Yes…' Emily said, and she heard the waver in her voice.

'Emily?' Eva checked, and made a gesture with her hand beneath her own chin, which told Emily to raise hers even higher. 'Better,' Eva said. 'You are confident, yes?'

'Yes,' she responded more firmly, and raised her chin a fraction higher.

And, indeed, she did feel more confident.

Flamenco was such an expressive dance, and somehow it made her more able to show her emotions, to examine her own feelings, even when she was away from the dance studio.

'Can I ask you a question?' she asked Alejandro that very night, as they lay in his gorgeous bed. 'Without you thinking I'm being all needy. I'm just curious, honestly…'

'Ask.'

'Why are you so closed off to relationships?'

'I don't want to rely on any one person.' He thought for a moment, then said, 'I don't think you can ever really rely on another person. You might think you can, but…' He turned his head on the pillow and looked at her. 'Look at you and your fiancé.'

'That was never love.' It was odd, but with Alejandro she could be honest—even with herself. 'I can see now that Gordon never loved me.'

'Did you love him?'

He asked the question lightly, in a way that said she didn't have to answer, but for Emily it brought a moment of self-examination as she thought back to their early days.

'No,' she admitted. 'I didn't know it, of course, but looking back I think I was so cooped up with caring for my dad that I just longed for the weekend and our nights out. I thought I loved Gordon when he was there for me after my father died, but…' She took a breath. 'No, I didn't love him.'

'Yet you stayed?'

'I did.' Emily nodded, scarcely able to believe that she'd set the bar to her happiness so low. 'It sounds weak, but after losing my parents I felt lost. He was always kind…'

'I'm not criticising,' Alejandro said. 'In fact, I can see why people might choose the safer option. It's a lot better than the rollercoaster of my parents' marriage.' He shook his head. 'How can you say you love someone when they cause you nothing but pain?'

'You mean your parents?'

'I would come home from school, or wherever, and they would be in the middle of a row. My father would be shouting and my mother would be throwing her clothes into her case. Sebastián would be angry… Carmen crying.' He screwed up his nose in distaste. 'I haven't thought of that in ages.'

'What about you?'

'I wanted to go on tour with her.' He gave a tight smile. 'She would say, "Next time, Alejandro." And then she'd point at me.' He did the same to Emily, pointing his finger in a warning gesture. 'And she would say, "Don't you cry, now."'

'Did you?'

'No.' He shook his head. 'I didn't want to add to it all. There was just too much drama and emotion. I never wanted that. I can remember telling my father to just stop…let her leave without a row…' He rolled his eyes. 'It was no wonder she didn't want to come back.'

Their nights were intimate and sexy. Discretion ruled the day, though. A feat far more easily achieved by Alejandro.

Emily's heart just leaped whenever she saw him, and it took all her restraint to give him only a vague wave if their paths crossed. And she kept forgetting— so much so that now, as he stared impassively at her bright smile on his computer screen, she wondered if her camera was on.

Rather quickly she worked out why his face was so bland when Sebastián's face dropped into the screen.

'Emile…' Sebastián said.

'Emily,' she corrected him nervously, and then smiled that bright smile. But it was a false one now, just so he wouldn't get a hint that she'd been smiling for his younger brother.

'We've had a first look at the new website,' he went on.

They approved of her work, it would seem, although Alejandro was definitely more effusive in the bedroom than during this, a business meeting, and Sebastián warned her that it wasn't a tourist guide to Jerez they wanted, and told her to focus more closely on the product.

'There's a photo shoot in the courtyard this afternoon?' Alejandro checked, and Emily realised that he was giving her a little prompt.

'Yes.' Emily nodded. 'All the courtyard images that are on the website now are placeholders. I'll be sure that the product is more prominent. Also, some of the images of the vineyards are being replaced with views from inside the restaurant. Ideally, I'd like a couple of images of you...'

'There are plenty.'

Sebastián was actually being helpful, perhaps because time was starting to race and she was still relying heavily on archive photos, because apart from Alejandro none of the family was particularly available.

'Actually, if you speak with the manager of the *taberna* he should have some old shots we were going to use for last year's summer festival.'

'I'll do that.' She took a breath. 'I was hoping to speak with Carmen about some images of her with the dancing horses...'

'Alejandro should have taken care of that,' said Sebastián.

He hadn't, though.

Despite a couple of prompts from Emily to meet his sister, a meeting had never materialised.

Now Alejandro gave his reasons. 'Carmen's not feeling particularly sociable at the moment.'

Sebastián rolled his eyes. 'I get it. But remind her the new website goes live in ten days.'

'Sure.' Alejandro nodded, then addressed Emily. 'Anything else?'

'They were my main questions.'

'Then if you can log out?' Alejandro responded. 'I would like to speak with Sebastián. Thank you for joining us.'

She'd been dismissed a little too harshly.

And Alejandro knew it.

He was trying not to show that there was anything going on with her to his brother, who knew him better than most. It was for the same reason he was avoiding introducing her to Carmen.

There was an electricity between himself and Emily that was hard to understand, let alone explain.

She lit him up.

There had been comments already about their first night in the *taberna*, sharing sherry and doing a tasting. It was something he had done many times; he hadn't considered it might draw attention. Yet people had noticed.

And they had noticed, too, how he'd intervened when she'd been being chatted up by Fernando.

So now he was attempting to halt them from becoming the talk of Jerez—and not just out of respect to Mariana. He was trying to shield Emily from the drama that would erupt if it was found out that they were seeing each other.

By keeping things secret he was trying to protect their increasingly diminishing days, and yet he knew Emily was getting irritated with being tucked away. She had asked him the other day if he was ashamed to be seen with her, and it had been so far off the mark that Alejandro had actually laughed.

'Why haven't you taken her to see Carmen?' Sebastián asked now.

'Because I have more on my mind than the new website and dancing ponies.' Alejandro shrugged and moved the subject back to Sebastián's stay in the States. 'How are the talks?'

'I'm headed to California tomorrow. Then back here to NYC in a couple of weeks. It would be great to have the new website by then... Or at least have them put up the old one.'

'No.' Alejandro would not be swayed. 'They've all seen the old one. This will launch by the due date.'

'Why are you so stubborn on this?'

It was because of the links to Mariana's family on the old site. The sherries the two companies shared, with more planned in the future. A personal future that had been designed with only the business in mind and one Alejandro didn't now want.

He buzzed his PA. 'Can you get Carmen to join us please?'

It took a while, but she came online and Alejandro told his siblings of his decision as far as the label went.

'I agree with Padre—we keep the original photo for the label.'

Maria de Luca's image would remain the face of the Romero sherry.

'I am also prepared to insist that she be included on the new website.'

'Why?' Sebastián demanded.

'Because our mother is a part of the Romero history—her first performance was here at the *taberna*.'

He had looked at both versions of Emily's work on this, and what he had seen had blown him away.

'You cannot tell our father's story by erasing our mother from the website. Although, of course, if that is what he wants I would stand by his choice.'

'Alejandro…' His older brother's face was as dark as thunder. 'The change was agreed months ago. *He* was the one who demanded it.'

'And then he found out how sick he is and changed his mind,' Alejandro pointed out. 'He wants to ensure Maria is taken care of.'

'I want her gone!' Carmen, his younger sister, sobbed.

But he would not allow her tears to move him, even if, out of all the siblings, Carmen had reason to hate their mother the most.

'It's all right for you—you were always her favourite,' his sister told him.

'Please…' He dismissed the notion. 'Anyway, it's not about us. It's about respecting our father's wishes. At the end of the day, it's a photograph on a bottle and a proper mention on the website—why would you let that bother you?'

'It's not just that. She's visiting him…she's at the hospital all the time, sneaking in after we've gone.'

'So what if she is?' Alejandro said. 'He loves her. What do you want to do—put guards on the door?'

'She's after his money.'

'Please,' Alejandro said again, once more dismissing the notion. 'She is one of Spain's most famous flamenco dancers. She has sell-out international tours even in her fifties…'

'You really believe she loves him?' Carmen snarled.

'Not for a moment—but it's what he wants to believe.'

'You know we'll just change it once he's gone,' Sebastián said. 'It will be two to one then.'

'Perhaps.' Alejandro stared at his older brother. 'But I haven't written him off as dead yet. Anyway, it's up to you if you want to disrespect his wishes.'

'Speaking of our father's wishes,' Sebastián said, 'what is happening with your wedding? We need a date...'

He spoke as if it were still a given—for both his and Mariana's family. The fact that they would one day marry had long been considered as such.

Alejandro didn't answer directly. 'I'm going to visit Padre this afternoon,' he informed his siblings. 'I'll tell him my decision about the label, and I also want to speak with his surgeon.'

Alejandro wanted to see his father for himself.

It was late afternoon when his plane landed in Madrid, and early evening by the time he'd spoken with the specialist before seeing his father.

'I don't want more surgery,' José said, and all Alejandro could think was how frail he looked.

But he did not address him as if he were—instead he chose to be blunt.

'Then do you want me to look at hospice care?' Alejandro asked. 'Because that is what all the specialists have said is the alternative. For the treatment to have any chance you need surgery...' He took a breath. 'Padre,' Alejandro said to this most difficult man, 'why are you not fighting?'

'I am,' he said.

'I have told Sebastián and Carmen that you have my vote for keeping Maria on the label, and I also agree she should be mentioned on the new website.'

'What did they say?'

'They are not best pleased.' Alejandro shrugged. 'But while you are still here there is little they can do. You can tell Maria the good news when she visits tonight… we all know she's here all the time.'

'Hmm…' His father let out a soft laugh. 'You don't approve?'

'It's not for me to approve.'

'She is talking of cancelling her summer tour to be with me.'

'So she'll take time off now you're dying? Are you worried she might not do it if you have a year or two left rather than months?'

'You sound like Sebastián.'

'No,' Alejandro said. 'Have you discussed surgery with her?'

It was a cruel question, perhaps, but had not been cruelly asked.

'No, I try to keep things light. She's seen enough of my moods.'

'Jesus…' Alejandro let out a soft laugh. His parents' relationship was toxic at best, fatal at worst—but then he had always known that. And so he sat on the bed and held his father's hand.

'I love her too much,' José said.

'No…' Alejandro shook his head, and looked around the luxurious private suite.

His father had everything he needed—Maria talking about cancelling her tour and visiting him. Sebastián and Carmen might hate her, but to Alejandro his father was as guilty in the breakdown of the marriage as she, and his summing up was an honest one.

'You would just do anything to keep her.'

'Alejandro, I want to make sure that the people I love are all taken care of.'

'I get that.'

'I think your wedding should take place sooner rather than later—' he started, but Alejandro cut in.

'I'm not marrying Mariana, Padre.'

'What are you talking about?'

'I shall support your business decisions, but you cannot dictate who and when I marry.'

'No! I have been patient, but it's time. I need to go to my grave knowing the future of the bodega is secure. And for that to happen—'

'Save the deathbed speeches,' Alejandro said. 'If you have the surgery there might be no need for them.' He would not be manipulated. 'I'm not going to marry on your command.'

Alejandro's voice halted as a rather too unfamiliar face peered around the door.

'Alejandro...' His mother gave a tight smile when she saw him. 'I didn't know you were here.'

'Since when do you ever know my plans?' He picked up his laptop and started to pack up.

'Don't rush off because of me, Alejandro.' She smiled at him.

'I have to fly back tonight.' Often he would stay on in Madrid, but on this night, after this exhausting day, he simply wanted to be at home.

'Alejandro has voted,' José told her. 'Your beautiful face shall stay on our label.'

'You voted for me?' Maria looked over to Alejandro and smiled in delight. 'You have always stood up for me.'

'I'm just respecting my father's wishes.'

'Not all of them,' said José. 'Alejandro, I'm asking you to reconsider. Take some time to think.'

'I don't want to reconsider,' Alejandro said. 'And I don't need time to think. I mean it, Padre. I have your back when it comes to the business, but just stay the hell out of my private life.'

The thought of home, with Emily, was tempting, and Alejandro flew through the late evening to be with her, rather than staying in a hotel.

Emily heard the soft knock on her door at what she guessed was around midnight. She lay there, trying not to be pathetic and jump out of bed just to greet him. He'd want her to go to his place, because her bed was too small for his frame.

It wasn't just because of his earlier cool treatment of her that she lay there. She'd actually felt a little ill after work…had just come home and gone to bed.

She was hurting, and she was worried she was going to get needy and mess up her side of the no-strings interlude to which they'd agreed.

He didn't knock twice.

And it should have come as a relief—except it did not.

She'd heard his PA book him a flight to Madrid and guessed he must be visiting his father.

Had there been bad news?

Hating herself for being so weak, she climbed out of bed and pulled on the rather tatty robe that he teased her about. Taking the key, she locked up.

He'd taught her the private code for his door, so she was able to slip in.

'Sorry about earlier,' he said as she entered his apartment. 'I just didn't want Sebastián getting wind of us.'

She didn't know what to say to that, so she said nothing.

'I went to visit my father,' he went on.

'I heard your PA calling the pilot to take you to Madrid. How is he?'

'At his manipulative best.'

And possibly so was his son. Because he peeled off his clothes and climbed into the vast wooden bed that had seen so much passion in recent weeks.

She wanted to be in his bed—that was why she'd come to him tonight. A little too easily, perhaps, but the damage to her pride was worth it.

Because he took her in a way he never had before.

He took her slowly, and held her arms above her head just to watch her orgasm.

'Alej...'

She was coming apart, and he was taking her as she did so, deeply kissing her, then pausing to softly kiss her eyes. And all the time he drove into her. Then he knelt up and held her hips as he took her to the limit, and the groan he let out as he achieved his own climax had her calling out as she orgasmed again more deeply than she ever had.

It was sex like she had never known existed.

Emily lay there in the dark, staring into the night and feeling Alejandro asleep, spooned into her, his arm over hers, his hand on her breast. And she didn't know any other way to describe the sex they'd just had.

It felt as if they had just made love.

CHAPTER TEN

'Hey!' Alejandro smiled as Emily came up the stairs carrying a large box. 'What the hell is that?'

'A flamenco doll,' Emily said, laughing as she opened up the door to her little apartment. 'I got it for Willow.'

'Your goddaughter?'

'Yes.'

He picked up the large boxed toy as she put it down and peered at the gaudy doll. She was dressed in a green frothy lace dress and her nails were painted red. There were plastic gold hoops in her ears.

'She's a bit creepy,' Alejandro said.

'Willow's four,' Emily said, by way of explanation. 'She'll love it. I've also bought her a dress to match.'

Emily had bought a lot of things for her goddaughter. Little sweets, a fridge magnet… It surprised him.

After all she was here working, not on holiday.

'Where are you going?' she asked. 'You're looking very smart.'

'I have a business lunch in Seville.'

'It's the weekend,' Emily said and he heard the slight strain to her tone.

It was her last weekend.

Her suitcase was out, and he hated the sight of it.

Usually it was tucked away in her wardrobe, but now and then she dragged it out, and he'd found it brought back too many memories.

Black memories that seemed to be becoming more vivid with each passing day.

His mother angrily throwing clothes in a suitcase as his father ripped them out.

Or the less eventful times…just coming downstairs in the morning and seeing the cases lined up, knowing that she was leaving again.

'I can come with you,' he remembered saying. 'I'll sit quietly.'

He'd often gone backstage, but as his mother's star had risen so too had the distances she travelled, and the number of after-parties and the demands of the tour.

'Not this time,' she would say. 'Next time, maybe?'

He'd sit quietly on the stairs, wishing his brother, who was five years older, would stop scowling, or his father would stop shouting, or the baby stop screaming…

'You're a good boy, Alejandro,' she'd say, as if in warning, and he'd halt the threatening tears and carry her handbag to the car.

Aside from staff, he'd been the only one to stand at the drive and wave her off. Smiling and waving while never knowing when or even if she'd be back.

He'd learned to turn his emotions off like a tap.

Yet he'd never mastered turning them back on.

He looked over to Emily, who gave him such a bright smile he was almost tempted to look over his shoulder to see who'd come in. But he knew that smile she wore only for him.

'Do you want to come with me to Seville?' he asked.

'To a business lunch?'

'No.' He pulled her towards him. 'That would not be very businesslike, but we could stay there for the night? Have dinner somewhere nice?'

There were nice places here in Jerez—beautiful, romantic places—yet he didn't take her to them, and not for the first time Emily found she had to bite her tongue.

She was growing tired of this endless discretion.

'You could go shopping,' he suggested, and named a very exclusive fashion house. 'I have an account there...'

'I can afford my own clothes, thank you!'

'Get your hair done, then,' he said.

It wasn't the first time he'd suggested it, and she knew he must have seen her expression.

'Or stay in bed...order champagne, or cake, or whatever. I thought most women loved to shop?'

'I don't.' Emily frowned. 'At least I don't think so.'

'I hate it,' he admitted, 'but I go there a couple of times a year and they make it as painless as possible. I'm just giving you options. It's up to you. But if you do want to come then we need to leave very soon.'

Emily wanted to go—and not just because she'd love to see Seville. It was simply the prospect of spending more time with Alejandro along with the prospect of a romantic night away.

Even if Alejandro insisted he didn't do romance, sometimes it felt exactly what this was.

'I'd love to come,' Emily admitted.

'Get ready then.' He glanced at her suitcase. 'You'll just need an overnight bag.'

Emily packed in a matter of moments. Her wardrobe was starting to fill with colour, but as she flung in a rather nice red top she'd purchased she paused and caught sight of herself in the wardrobe mirror. Despite her wishing he'd take her somewhere nice here, even if he offered she had nothing suitable to wear.

God, maybe she did need a wardrobe update.

Or was it that he was embarrassed to be seen out with her?

'Hey!' He was waiting in the car to take her out for their unexpected adventure, and smiled when she got in. 'I just have to drop into the equestrian school. I need to leave some brochures for Carmen.'

'Can I meet her?' Emily said. 'I still haven't taken any photos of her.'

'You found some, though.'

'Yes, but I'd love to speak to her, and I do want to see the equestrian school.'

'Another day,' Alejandro said. 'I'm just dropping these off. We don't have time to stop.'

There never was time to stop, but instead of dwelling on the elusive Carmen, she told him her news.

'I've got two new clients,' Emily said. 'Well, one's paid a deposit.'

'That's great. You're building their websites?'

'Yes.'

'What sort of businesses are they?'

'A sports centre in the North of England.' Well, it was an indoor bowling centre…and the other was an MOT and tyre replacement franchise. 'And I've got a craft beer company who've made a couple of enquiries.'

'That's great.'

'I don't know how I'm going to pretend to like beer.'

'Were you pretending about the sherry?'

'You'll never know!'

He smiled at her teasing as they pulled in at the equestrian school. 'I'd know,' he said, and gave her a quick kiss before heading into the building.

She waited in the car, but the place was simply too beautiful to ignore and soon she climbed out, looking at the glorious mustard-yellow and white building, itching to go inside and find out more about the famous dancing horses.

Gosh, there was so much to explore and to see…six weeks was never going to be enough time. She doubted a full year would be enough.

It was her time with Alejandro that had especially raced by, though.

'Couldn't resist,' Emily said, and he smiled as he walked towards her and saw she was taking photos. And, no, she couldn't resist. As he approached her she took some shots of him.

God, he was beautiful.

He continued to walk towards her, his suit in the bright sun almost like liquid on his long limbs. And then he made her laugh, because he took off his jacket and threw it over one shoulder, then gave her a look, as if he were strutting down the catwalk.

'Work it, baby…' she said, and that made him laugh too. He pouted his lips and strutted, and she laughed so much she possibly took more photos of the ground and the sky than of him.

'Alejandro…'

A woman, who could only be Carmen, was calling him. She had the same beautiful bone structure and the same effortless grace as she ran to catch up with her brother.

'What are you here for?'

'Carmen…'

His laughter quickly dropped away, Emily noticed.

'I've just dropped off some brochures, as I told you I would.'

'So why not stop by and say hello?' she asked in Spanish.

'Because I have to be in Seville by midday.'

Carmen was slender, dressed in jodhpurs and a black T-shirt and boots. Though tiny, her stance was confident and her dark eyes suspicious, and her question as she glanced over towards Emily was direct.

'Quién es ella?' Carmen asked—*'Who is she?'*

'This is Emily,' Alejandro said in English. 'Emily, this is my sister Carmen…'

'Buenos días,' Emily said.

The greeting wasn't returned.

'Emily is doing the new website.'

'Just the new website?' Carmen said. 'Or one of the Romero brothers too?'

'Hey…' Alejandro warned his sister, but it didn't stop Carmen.

'Does Mariana know?' she asked, again in Spanish.

'Don't even go there, Carmen,' he told her.

'Clearly she doesn't know, if you're heading to Seville. Isn't that where you hide all your lovers?'

'No one's hiding.'

'Why do people have to lie?' Carmen sobbed, and then turned on her heel and ran off.

Alejandro stood there, shaking his head. Then he turned and must have seen Emily's stricken face.

'Did you understand all that?' he asked.

'I think so.' She felt a little sick, in fact. 'Am I being hidden?'

'Don't be ridiculous,' he snapped, and they got back in the car and drove in silence.

Alejandro could feel the tension in Emily and he addressed it. 'You think I'm hiding you because I'm still seeing Mariana. But I told you right at the start we'd broken up. I confided in you.'

She stared ahead but didn't respond.

'Say it—whatever it is you're thinking. Because if you don't fight your corner, Emily, then no one else will…'

She clearly did not know how to, though.

'So we drive in silence.' He shrugged.

Fast too.

She pulled down the sun visor and tried to ready herself for the hotel in Seville. To make matters worse there was a shiny red bump on her chin—when she'd stopped getting spots by the time she was sixteen.

She could see the signs for Seville now, and suddenly not only had she been invited to address the situation, she wanted to. She was so tired of ignoring her own insecurities.

'Have you told Mariana that it's over?'

'As I've already told you—yes. I told her in December, and then I told her to make it public the very night that you and I met.'

'But she hasn't?'

'Not to my knowledge.'

'And you haven't told your brother or your sister?'

'I'm thirty-one years old. I don't need their advice

or their take on things. I have been quite busy, in fact, since the so-called break-up…' He glanced over. 'Why do you think I'm lying?'

'Because I *do* feel hidden.' She screwed her eyes closed. 'We don't go out together…'

'We've been together for three weeks,' Alejandro said. 'And we've spent all our time in bed.' He looked over at her. 'Do you want us to make out at work?'

'No!'

Emily was unused to a row.

Or rather she was unused to a row with passion.

'I feel…' She didn't know what to say—or rather knew that if she did say anything it would be too much.

She was crazy about him. She was trying to tell herself it was just fun, a little holiday romance, only she craved more.

And if he was cheating on Mariana then at least she could end it, start to hate him, rather than feeling this wave of emotion that had been building since the second they had met. Emotion she was trying to contain, to push down.

Because she wanted him all the time. She wanted to know about his father, his family, his sister… She wanted more involvement than he did.

'You feel…?' he invited as they entered the city of Seville.

Its stunning architecture would have taken her breath away on any other day, but she saw it now through tear-filled eyes, turning her head so as to not let him see.

He drove expertly through the heavy traffic, with her his tense, silent partner… Finally, she spoke. 'I feel like a secret.'

'We agreed to keep things discreet.'

'No, you told me that was how it would be,' Emily said, the floodgates opening and a lifetime of insecurities finally being given voice. 'Are you ashamed to be seen with me?'

'Where the hell did *that* come from?' He looked genuinely perplexed.

'You're the most demonstrative man I've ever met, but only when we're in private.' Emily was as close to shouting as she had ever come. She so badly wanted to believe him, but knew she was being fed lies. 'You don't want a relationship—I get that. You couldn't have made it any clearer. And now you're suggesting I buy a new wardrobe.'

'Because you so often say you have nothing to wear.'

'And you want me to get my hair cut.'

'Every morning you complain about your hair. You told me you cut it yourself. I thought it might feel nice?'

'Hair salons are a waste of money.'

They were pulling into a hotel forecourt. Doormen were leaping forward, whistles were blowing as Alejandro's car came to a halt. And so too did her heart as she choked out a question.

'Are you embarrassed to be seen with me?'

'Emily...'

'Am I not sophisticated enough?'

She didn't await his answer.

As the doorman opened the passenger side Emily leaped out.

For a full moment he sat there, gripping the steering wheel, stunned at their row. He'd never cared enough to row before, and he never invited drama in.

Alejandro was appalled, too, that in trying to shield

Emily from the wrath of both his and Mariana's family if their affair was exposed he'd made her feel like some grubby secret.

He looked up to where she stood, delving in her bag for a tissue, apologising and stepping out of the way as some arrogant hotel guests brushed past.

Alejandro would have liked to get out and tap her on the shoulder, correct her on one vital point...

It was Emily who was embarrassed by herself, Emily who apologised if another person stepped on her shadow. Emily who would rather buy gifts for others than spend anything on herself. And, for all there was much to address from her outburst—Mariana, his family, work—it was the evidence of her insecurities that had shaken him the most.

And those were the first things he would address.

His way, though.

There was no checking in required at the opulent hotel—they knew him well—but as they took the ancient elevator to his suite there was an explosive energy between them.

The elevator pinged. Emily didn't even look at the suite they stepped directly into—just stood there as Alejandro dismissed the butler.

'You don't come near me when we're out and I don't get why,' she said suddenly.

'You want to know why?'

Oh, he was going to come near her now.

'Because I have recently broken up with someone. And even if there was no love there, there was respect. Do you think it would be fair for her to hear that we're together?'

Emily caught her breath.

'Do you think it would be kind for us to be seen dancing in the *taberna*…' he pulled her in '…like this? Pressing in to each other?' He lifted her hair and deeply kissed her neck, touched her as he wanted to all the time. *All the time.* 'If you think I'm a cheat you're wrong about that, and if you think I'm ashamed or embarrassed by you, then you might as well go. Because that means you don't know me at all.' He looked right at her. 'I think you're beautiful.'

'You're just saying that.'

'Why would I just say that? I want you all the time.' He watched her rapid blink, and the pinch of her lips as she fought his compliments. 'I don't want others to find out because I want to protect you for what little time we have.'

'Protect me from what?'

'If my family thought you were the reason for Mariana and I breaking up you would be hated.' He looked at her. 'And you don't deserve to be.'

'Hated?' she checked.

'At the very least you would be blamed. I'm trying to protect you. Protect *us*,' he elaborated. 'We have a week left, and I don't want my family or Mariana's to spoil a single moment of our time.'

'Why would they spoil it?'

'My father still wants to see a marriage between Mariana and me—even more so since he fell ill. I've told him it won't be happening. I just don't want him, or anyone, to think you're the reason why it isn't going ahead.'

'So *why* isn't it going ahead?' Emily asked. 'I mean, if the land and the business are so important, and you don't care for love…'

He was knotting his tie, and as his hand paused on the heavy silk he hoped she didn't notice that he faltered.

He met Emily's eyes in the mirror and answered her question honestly. 'I couldn't promise that I'd remain faithful for the rest of my life.'

Alejandro watched Emily blink, and her lips pinch in distaste at his response, and he wanted to amend his answer—*I couldn't promise Mariana that I'd be faithful for the rest of my life. But I could promise you...*

It was as if the mirror had cracked before his eyes—the mental correction was completely at odds with his usual thinking. And absolutely not what they had agreed.

'That's a very good reason not to marry,' she said.

'Yes.'

He turned from the mirror and looked at Emily.

She hid herself from the world, but not from him. She was like a star, glinting and starting to brighten in a night sky, and he wanted her to soar.

Alejandro wanted more for her than barely formed promises he didn't believe in nor know how to keep. He wanted her to take her newly discovered self from his bedroom out into the world. For her to know she could stand up for herself and fight her corner. To know, as he had the day they met, that she was beautiful, talented and funny.

'Emily, I have kept things quiet because of the reaction of my family and Mariana's. Not because of you.'

She nodded, but he could still see the shadow of doubt in her eyes and knew he had to do more to convince her. So he turned back to the mirror and pulled his hair forward.

'You know what? You're right.'

* * *

'About what?'

Emily was trying to keep her voice steady and hide her disappointment at his response, reminding herself that he'd said from the start he didn't do long-term relationships.

'About cutting your own hair. A professional salon is not just a waste of money,' Alejandro said. 'It's a waste of time. Every two weeks I have to sit in that chair getting this trimmed. It's due now.'

She tried to drag her mind from fidelity to hair, from his family's wrath to the business lunch he was getting ready to attend…

'You look fine,' she said, when in reality he looked perfect, with his dark suit, his silver tie, and his hair that didn't look as if it was due a cut. But then that thick, glossy hair was always superbly styled, his sideburns neatly trimmed. Of course there was some serious grooming going on.

And then she saw him pulling a few strands of hair down and delving in his toiletry bag. He took out some small nail scissors.

'What are you doing, Alejandro?'

'I told you—I'm due for a trim…' He took a chunk of black silky hair, right at the front.

He was teasing…she was sure.

Oh, no!

'Stop it!'

'Why?' He hacked into his fringe and she watched open-mouthed as several inches of black hair fell to the floor. 'See?' he said. 'Nothing to it.'

'Alejandro!'

'What?' He frowned. 'Don't you like it?'

'It's…'

It was dreadful. More than that, she couldn't believe he would do that just to make a point. And as he stood there, still impossibly beautiful, to her utter surprise Emily found she'd started to laugh, and so had he.

'You cannot go out like that.'

'Why not?' he demanded.

'Let me fix it.' She reached for the scissors but his hand closed over hers.

'Oh, no,' he said. 'I've seen your handiwork. Anyway, if my hair is so awful that you don't want to be seen with me tonight, then we can get room service.'

'Don't be ridiculous…' Emily's voice trailed off as she realised what she had just said—it was *ridiculous* to suggest that she wouldn't want to be seen with him because of his hair.

'Get it?' he said, and lifted her chin so that she looked into those beautiful eyes.

Finally she nodded.

'I think you're beautiful,' he said. 'I just wish we were in agreement.'

'I feel guilty,' she admitted in truth. 'I feel guilty spending money.'

'Spend mine, then.' He smiled and kissed her briefly, hard on the mouth. 'I'll see you after this lunch,' Alejandro said. 'Although it might go on for a while.'

'Sure…' As he picked up the swipe card and went to go, she halted him with a statement. 'Alejandro, I don't care if your family hate me.'

'I do,' he said. 'My family don't always play nice.'

He left her then.

Only Emily no longer felt as if she was being hidden. She dug into her handbag and took out the amber seal. She held it between her fingers and up to the light, looking at the little trapped butterfly wing. She thought of Alejandro, chopping off his beautiful hair just to make a point to her. She thought of their row, and the way she'd voiced her fears and been listened to when she had.

Emily almost expected the amber resin to crack and the little wing to fly off.

She felt a little more free...

Seville really was incredible—she could easily see why Alejandro chose to spend a lot of time here. The architecture was stunning, and she visited the cathedral and then walked through a park. The scent of orange blossom was heavy in the air and it was, despite everything she'd heard, just a bit too sickly-sweet for her taste.

And then she found herself back at the hotel and in the hair salon, rather hoping she'd be told there were no appointments. But she was soon sitting in a seat with a black cape around her shoulders.

'Just a little,' she said, on constant repeat, but she was suitably ignored as layers were added to her hair.

She almost didn't care. She just closed her eyes and told herself she could not be in love with a man who didn't feel capable of being faithful to his wife.

Just enjoy the time you have, she kept telling herself.

And, despite feeling teary, she *was* enjoying herself. Every second of their time was to be treasured, because even their row had been a revelation—she could say what she was thinking, fight her corner, state her case. She simply couldn't imagine doing so with another man.

'Señorita?'

She opened her eyes, surprised by her own reflection. Her hair was still the same length, yet now it fell in ringlets, and the cotton wool ends had gone.

The style brought out natural highlights and, even if it was fiercely expensive, apart from her camera she knew it was the best money she had ever spent.

She felt braver, somehow. And, given she'd hardly ever spent money on clothes, she walked into the boutique he'd recommended.

'Señorita...'

She had a feeling Alejandro might have alerted them to expect her, because they were so ridiculously nice.

She was offered champagne, which she declined, and opinions and gentle suggestions, some of which she accepted.

There was a gorgeous red dress that felt like too much, and a pale lilac one that washed her out.

'I don't know what colours suit me,' Emily admitted. 'I tend to wear grey and black.' She knew that made her sound boring. 'And navy,' she added.

'What colour do you like best?'

'Brown,' she answered without thinking, just imagining Alejandro's eyes. 'But that's not a colour. I suppose I need bright...'

'No, no! Wear what you love!'

As it turned out, chocolate-brown *was* a colour.

The dress was very simple, with a scoop neck and bias cut, and it fell to the knee and made her curves look curvy rather than... Well, rather than making her want to hide them.

Was this what love did? Emily wondered.

It was her first true acknowledgement that she'd been deluding herself.

She was crazy about Alejandro.

Head over heels in love with him.

She knew then why she'd almost shouted in anger before…why she'd been shaking as she'd confronted him.

Because she was angry with herself.

It was she who was lying in this relationship.

She who was breaking their rules.

Emily utterly and completely loved him.

And it would ruin their last days if he knew.

She went a little wild…bought the shoes that matched the dress and a small handbag too.

'Thank you,' she said, as she took out her credit card, and saw the assistant's slight frown.

Ah, so Alejandro had indeed called ahead.

But no. She didn't need him to buy her clothes. She had just needed a nudge to do so, and she knew that never, ever would she be in this position again.

Never, ever would she walk through Seville on a bright spring day, knowing she would be with Alejandro tonight.

Never, ever would she turn down an itty-bitty lane and peer into an antiques shop window, stare at the cover of a flamenco record leaning on an old gramophone. Instead of showing a colourful female dancer, it was the shadowy silhouette of a man by an open fire.

It could almost be Alejandro, Emily thought.

It wasn't, of course—the vinyl was far too old for that. But it was enough to propel her into the shop.

'Excepcional…' the owner told her, letting her know it was rare, but it wasn't that, nor even the gorgeous cover, that had her entranced.

As she looked at the track list she was sure there was

a version of the song they had danced to on the night they had first made love.

It was too much, Emily thought, putting the record down. Though for once it wasn't the cost she was wrestling with, but the gesture. It was too romantic, she told herself, and she thanked the owner and moved to walk out.

Anyway, Alejandro had a huge record collection, and he could afford anything…

But she wanted to give him a gift.

Something from her.

To him.

She turned around.

'Me gustaría comprar esto.' 'I'd like to buy this.'

No, never again would she be walking along the balcony of a Moorish palace, excited by her purchase, wondering about his reaction, feeling like an Arabian princess who would be with her prince tonight. Looking up at the mosaic tiling and soaring arches, and then down to the maze of plants beneath…

And wondering how not to cry.

How to get through the upcoming days and somehow hide the love she'd just acknowledged—but only to herself.

She was nervous as she crossed the hotel foyer. Worried that her silent admission might be blazing in her eyes. And there he was, shaking hands with his lunch date, so she held back, not wanting to disturb them.

But he looked over—and then looked again.

'Good God!' He gave her a smile as he came over. 'I just had to give myself a quick talking-to. I saw this gorgeous blonde smiling at me and had to remind myself that you were upstairs and I'd promised you a month of commitment.'

'You did.' She started to laugh.

'Then I realised it was you...' He ran a hand down the silky curls and toyed with them. 'You!' He looked at her. 'I think we're good for each other. Because *you* are smoking hot and *I've* just nailed a deal I've been chasing for two years.'

'Seriously?'

'Yes,' he said as they made their way up to their suite. 'He's usually terrible at small talk, but he asked what had happened to my hair...' His mouth came down to hers. 'I told him I'd tried to cut it myself. Talk about opening the floodgates... Apparently he shaved his eyebrows off when he was ten...'

She was laughing as he took out the swipe card and they went into the suite where they'd previously rowed. Although she put down most of her bags, she held on to one.

'I got you this.'

'What is it?'

'Just a...' She felt nervous, unsure if it was too little for a billionaire, or too much for a brief romance as he pulled the record from its wrapping. 'I saw it and I thought of you. You've probably already got it...'

'No...' He was reading the back of the cover. 'We danced to this.'

'Yes.' She gave a slightly nervous laugh as he turned the record over in his hands. 'He looks like you,' she said. 'Well, a bit. I just saw it...'

For once, Alejandro did not know what to say.

She'd floored him.

On a day that had clearly been about her she had stopped and thought of him.

He thought of the doll for her goddaughter, the handbag for her friend and how she stopped in the midst of a busy day and thought of others.

It meant more than he dared admit.

'Thank you,' he said, worried that if he said more he might say too much.

Emily was watching him as he put the record down, as if trying to gauge his reaction.

He took her face in his hands and looked at her, and then ran his fingers through her curls.

He looked at all the changes—not so much the make-up and the hair, but the fact that she'd gone and done it. Then he turned her around so that she faced the mirror, and he slowly, carefully, removed the dress and placed it over a chair.

She stood in rather disappointing underwear, considering her transformation, but he didn't care about that at all.

'Stay there.'

Emily stood, watching him move behind her and feeling his fingers as he unhooked her bra. She watched her breasts drop a little, and then his hands peeled down her knickers.

'Alejandro...'

She turned her head, aching for his mouth, or at least his touch, but he was undressing now, placing his clothes on the chair, and then he came and stood behind her again.

She watched him toy with her breasts, rolling the

nipples into indecent lengths, and then he moved his hands down, and she watched him stroke her.

'Face me,' he said, and she did so.

She looked at the dark hair on his chest and his mahogany nipples and she kissed one, feeling it salty on her lips. He smelt of cologne, and now he was pulling her into him, wanting to lift her.

'I want to watch us…' he said, but she refused to scale that magnificent body and instead dropped to her knees.

'Watch this…' she said.

It was the first time she'd taken him in her mouth because, despite the fact he'd tasted every inch of her, there were still things she hadn't tried.

And this was one.

She'd felt too naïve before, too gauche to attempt it, but now she knew she wasn't being judged, that it was just sheer pleasure they gave to each other.

'God…' he moaned as she kissed up his dark length and came to the tip.

He was tall, so he hooked the chair with his foot and brushed off all the lovely folded clothes, letting her sit down.

'Hold it,' he said, lifting her glossy curls so he could see her hands and her face and her lips around his length. He guided her hand for a moment, and then he stopped and sank into the pleasure of her untutored mouth working him.

He started to thrust and then attempted not to.

She pulled her head back and looked at him, all gleaming and wet from her mouth, and then she took him in her mouth again, a little more boldly. Her bottom was lifting off the seat as he started to thrust. Her own sex was hot as she took him more deeply than she'd ever thought she'd dare.

He was brushing her hair from her face, tucking it behind her ear, tender with his hands. And he was no longer watching in the mirror, just tending to her as she tended to him.

'Emily…'

His voice held a warning, and she could feel him swelling in her mouth, and then he shouted a breathless shout, and she tasted him for the first time, stunned at the pleasure of this intimacy, taut and on the edge of coming herself as she looked up at him, so glad for these moments.

'Come here,' he told her.

He pulled her up and took her to bed, and they lay silent together, wrapped in their own thoughts but not sharing them.

She knew it might be a little dangerous to do that.

CHAPTER ELEVEN

IT WASN'T JUST the brilliant sex, or the walking hand in hand to the restaurant, it was the long slow dinner, where the waiter kept having to come back because neither was ready to order.

'You look incredible.'

Alejandro took Emily's hand in the candlelight. The white tablecloth was dotted with little gold foil stars and, feeling his hand over hers, she felt the happiest she ever had.

'And with that curly hair you won't have to get it done again for ages.'

'How do you know that?'

'I'm not sure…' He shrugged. 'Perhaps I read it.'

'Or one of your lovers told you?'

'God, no, they're always at the hair salon,' he said. 'Not you, though?'

He sounded curious, rather than scathing, enough that she shook her head and told him how her mother had always cut her hair.

'She made all my clothes too.'

'Seriously?'

'She was very talented at sewing and knitting.' She felt a surge of tears, out of place on such a gorgeous night, but his hand simply held hers and he allowed her to speak on. 'I don't think my teenage self appreciated that at the time.'

'You wanted high fashion?'

'Yes,' Emily admitted. 'But now I feel so dreadful for all the times I sulked when she made me yet another jumper…' She gave a shrill laugh. 'She made me a pair of jeans once. They were awful, and I told her so.' He held her hand tighter. 'I'd give anything to have a pair of her hand-made jeans or one of her jumpers now.'

'It sounds as if you had incredible parents.'

'I did,' Emily agreed. 'I just didn't always appreciate it at the time.'

'Emily…' He sounded both practical and kind. 'You just wanted to fit in.'

She nodded, thinking of how she'd been teased, growing up, about her clothes, her hair… And how she'd always wanted to protect her mother.

'I feel guilty.' She reached into her new handbag, but of course there were no tissues, so she had to dab her eyes with the heavy serviette and she felt him watching. 'I don't expect you to get it.'

'You don't think I know about guilt?'

'I didn't mean it like that.' She looked over at him. 'You feel guilty too?'

He nodded, and told her that things were strained with his siblings. 'We've been arguing,' he admitted.

'Since you came down on your father's side about the label and Maria in his bio?'

'No, since my father grew ill.'

He poured wine for himself and held the bottle up for her, but Emily declined. She just wanted to hear about him.

'The three of us are so different, but we have always been.' Putting down the bottle, he laced his fingers and gripped his hands together. 'We are tight-knit. At least we were—now we argue.'

'About…?'

'My mother visiting my father…getting more medical opinions. I was taking Carmen some brochures for a hospice…'

'Alejandro…' Her face fell. 'I didn't realise it had come to that.'

'It hasn't,' he said. 'Although if he doesn't have surgery, it soon shall. Carmen and I are trying to jolt him into action.' He gave a thin smile. 'We all used to get on better, but since my father fell ill we seem to argue over everything.'

'That's good,' Emily said.

He frowned at her words. 'Good?'

'I wish I'd had siblings—especially when my father was so ill and confused. I would have loved someone to argue a point with me. I just felt so responsible—that every decision was mine and mine alone.'

'I hadn't thought of it like that.'

'At least you all want the best for him—you just have different views as to what that is. Still, it sounds as if the choices are his.'

'Yes.' He nodded. 'He's not confused or anything.'

Then he told her something she already knew, but she felt very privileged to hear it from him.

'My mother has started to visit him in the hospital. Sebastián and Carmen think it's just for his money.'

'Do you?'

'No.' He dismissed the notion out of hand. 'I pointed out to them that she is still on tour, even in her late fifties… I know she's extremely comfortable.' He thought for a long moment. 'She is also incredibly vain, and likes having her photo on the Romero product.'

'Yet she never took his name?' Emily frowned. 'Or is de Luca a stage name?'

'No, it's different here. Wives don't take their husband's name, but the children take both their parents'… My full name is Alejandro Romero de Luca.'

'Did you drop your mother's name because of the divorce?'

'No.' He was clearly trying to explain the complicated system to Emily, who hadn't grown up with it. 'You are addressed by your paternal surname, so I am Señor Romero. Given the business side of things, for me it is more prominent.'

'Oh…' She hadn't known that. 'So Sebastián and Carmen are Romero de Luca too?'

'Si.' He nodded.

'But what happens when you have children?'

'Never.' He shuddered at the very thought, and certainly didn't explain further. So much so, she thought, that rather than enlighten her as to the surname of his hypothetical babies, he called for the dessert menu.

'I can't decide…' Emily admitted.

'I already have,' Alejandro told her. 'Tocino de Cielo. It is like your crème caramel—you remember how I told you sherry was clarified with egg white?'

'I think so…' Emily nodded, because it was rather difficult to remember anything when she was locked in his gaze.

'Well, they used to give the unused egg yolks to the local nuns, and they came up with this dessert. It's very traditional in these parts…'

'Nuns made this?'

'They still do. We could go to Acros de la Frontera on the way home, and if you like it we can stop at the convent and get more.'

It really was the most delicious dessert—as well as the most gorgeous night.

When it ended she scooped up the little gold stars from the table and put them in a pouch in her bag.

'For Willow?' he said.

'Yes.' She nodded, except she knew she might have to keep these little gold stars for herself, along with the amber resin from the sherry bottle.

Only she didn't want them to be mere memories… an amber and gold shrine kept to remind her of him.

He took her to Plaza de España and they strolled across the bridges and stood by the water fountain. It was stunning, with ceramic-tiled bridges and even seats, all blues and yellows. For once Emily was glad not to have her camera with her. Oh, she'd come back and take photos, but on this night it was just so nice to walk hand in hand and take it all in.

It was only when they were walking back to the hotel that she felt him tense. His stride slowed for a brief second, but he said nothing and carried on walking, though she quickly saw why.

There was a poster—one of many pasted onto the wall. But Maria de Luca certainly stood out. She was so stunning and beguiling that Emily couldn't pretend not to have seen it—in fact she herself had already slowed down.

'Your mother's performing here?'

'No, I think that's an old poster.'

They wandered over to read it, but Emily was right.

His mother was performing this weekend in Seville. It was a chance, the poster read, to see her before she headed off on an international tour.

Alejandro looked at his mother, smiling for any passing stranger, or for patrons who were willing to drop a couple of hundred euros to see her perform.

Maria de Luca.

Loved, revered and adored.

Just rarely at home.

And when she had been she'd simply been filling time before she went away again.

'She never bought us gifts when she went away,' he said.

'I'm sure she was busy...'

'Come off it, Emily—you're working twelve-hour days, and putting in extra at night. You're cramming in dance lessons, sleeping with me...' He refused to make excuses for his mother. 'You're only Willow's godmother, yet you still make the time to call her, to bring back gifts, you think of her.'

'Yes...'

'And you thought of me today.'

'Of course,' she said. 'It might only be a holiday romance, but you'll always be my first lover, Alejandro.'

Her words brought him little comfort, though.

First? This night he wanted to amend her words, to kiss her against the wall and correct her, tell Emily that he would be her *only* lover.

Who was he to hold her back, though?

CHAPTER TWELVE

THE WEBSITE LOOKED INCREDIBLE.

The photo she had taken of Alejandro that first morning was the site's main image and her favourite.

They hadn't even kissed then, Emily thought as she sat at her desk in this her final week working for the Romeros.

It felt too soon to be leaving.

So much so that she'd secretly considered forgoing her bonus just to delay things. But then, Emily had told herself, she'd actually be paying for the pleasure of more time with him.

No.

Anyway, she doubted Alejandro would appreciate it.

Things had been a little strained between them since their dinner on Saturday night, in a way she couldn't quite define.

Yes, they'd made love, and on the Sunday he'd driven her to Acros de la Frontera, where they'd bought more of the sweet dessert they'd enjoyed from the nuns, but she'd fallen asleep on the car ride home.

He'd woken her as they'd approached Jerez and asked if she was looking forward to going home, and she'd looked at the city, spread before them, and felt a little ill at the thought of leaving…

Or had she simply been car sick?

She'd taken a drink from her water bottle and looked at the cathedral and the *alcázars*, the ancient buildings and the streets she loved to wander…

How did she tell a man who wanted no strings that this place felt like home?

How did she tell a man who didn't believe in love that she had fallen in love with him on sight?

Emily knew now that she had lied from the start.

It had always been love.

But instead of telling him that she'd told him how excited she was to return home. To see Willow and Anna and face the new challenges that awaited her, and how she was already sorting out dates with the trye replacement company.

'Tyres?' he'd said, and she hadn't been able to define his tone.

A little derogatory?

Or had he just been bewildered?

She wasn't sure.

'It will be brilliant,' Emily had told him, taking another sip of water as she thought of all that rubber and oil and tried to be upbeat. 'You know, I thought sherry was an old ladies' drink before I came to Jerez,' she'd said brightly. 'I'm sure that tyres…'

She'd given in then, unable to face the fact that her time here was almost done. Wondering if she should admit she'd given herself two weeks' leave at the end of this trip. Unsure if he'd welcome the news.

And so rather than feign delays, Emily had just got on with her work.

Yet there were so many memories on the website. The written pages were lined with pictures of the intricate laced vines in the courtyard that she'd taken while lying down.

She forced herself to click past that page. To turn her attention to an image of José and Maria on their wedding day, the gorgeous couple dancing in the courtyard. There was also a beautiful, previously unseen image of Maria, performing flamenco in the *taberna*.

Even without Carmen's input Emily had found a photograph of her on a gorgeous black Andalusian horse, riding through the vineyards. Sebastián though, was proving harder. There were no smiling faces where he was concerned, nor casual shots that she could easily find.

But today, at the eleventh hour, Emily had come across one. He was on the rooftop terrace, with the sun setting behind him, the church spire in the background, and he was toasting a stunning woman. Both were holding up sherry glasses, and even the bottle had the label facing the right way.

Emily was almost shaking when she found the perfect shot. It was just a couple of days before the website went live.

She called Alejandro's office.

'I've found a photo of Sebastián…' She described it. 'It has everything.'

'God, no,' he said, almost instantly. 'Just forget you even saw that.'

'But it has the bottle, the sherry, the sunset and the spire…'

'That is him and Isabel.'

'Isabel?' Emily frowned. She'd never heard that

name, and there was a bitter note to Alejandro's tone.
'Who's she?'

'Sebastián's reluctant ex. That was taken when they
had just got engaged. It all fell apart a couple of weeks
later.'

'Why?'

But Alejandro wasn't about to enlighten her. 'Seriously, Emily,' he warned, 'don't even go there.'

Emily sighed. 'Okay. There is another one of him on
the same photo shoot. It's just Sebastián, with his back
to the wall. He's holding a glass, but it doesn't show the
bottle... He looks incredible.'

It was almost as good. Actually, it was just as good,
as the amber sherry reflected the sunset and glinted
like liquid gold.

'Can I use that?' she asked.

'Send a copy over to me and I'll discuss it with him.'
He sounded distracted. 'I'm meeting with him soon. I'll
see what he says.'

Emily did so, and then spent a good couple of hours
with her translator, who was, thankfully, pedantic. She
could see now why Alejandro had insisted that she write
in English, because the translator managed to convey
things she could not.

'*Sobremesa,*' he said now. 'Sitting with family and
friends after a heavy meal, just relaxing and talking.'

'Perfect.'

It was so exciting, seeing her photos come to life
with the words beside them. And who knew that *con-
cuño* or *concuña* meant the spouse of an in-law, which
helped so much to shorten the descriptions on ancient
family photos.

Romero tradition and history went way back. It was

something that she pondered on as she made her way to her lunchtime dance class. It was to be followed by another one to one with Eva, as she was trying to cram in as many as she could before she left Jerez.

Before she left…

She felt the days peeling away, as if the wind had caught the paper of a calendar and was simply blowing their time away.

As she waited for the group class to conclude Emily eyed the wall chart and tried to see if there were any more classes she could take, and when her private class commenced she asked Eva about it.

'I have my male class,' Eva said. 'Okay, now footwork…' She was clearly able to keep two conversations going at the same time. 'You are welcome to join in.'

'I don't think so.' Emily's confidence had indeed come on, but she wasn't ready to take a lesson in front of a group of men. Still, it was interesting to think of men taking classes.

'Faster!' Eva said. '*Tacón, tacón, tacón, golpe*! Put some anger into it…'

Emily tried, but even after weeks of faithful practice, and lots of expert tuition by Alejandro, Emily simply couldn't get her body to express itself in the way she wanted. Oh, it was improving, but she still felt like a wooden doll compared to the other women.

'Did you teach Alejandro?' Emily asked, taking a quick drink of water. It was hard doing footwork and holding a shawl.

'Teach?' Eva laughed. 'Well, I suppose you could call it that…' She saw Emily's frown in the mirror. 'Oh, you mean flamenco…' She gave her a smile. 'No, I never taught him that.'

Emily's face was as bright as the practice skirt she wore. Even her arms were blushing as she raised them when Eva did. Then the teacher struck the floor with her full foot and Emily started to *palma*...

'Come on, now, Emily.'

Emily met Eva's eyes and gave in with light palmas and matched her foot strike. It felt good to stamp.

To stamp for her jealousy and at the *ick* factor that here was another of Alejandro's lovers, and he clearly remained friendly with her.

Would he with her?

The question was immaterial, Emily quickly realised—very soon she wouldn't be here.

They were down to their final days...

Actually, as Alejandro was just finding out, they were down to their final hour.

'How is Padre?' Sebastián asked after their father at the beginning of their online meeting.

Alejandro could hear the strain in his older brother's voice. Usually they spoke first about work, and got that out of the way before addressing family matters, but their father's health was the first topic Sebastián raised.

'He's much the same as when you left,' Alejandro informed him. 'He's still refusing surgery, but I think he's starting to understand that is his only choice.'

'So why are we looking at hospices?'

Alejandro turned his pen up and down on his desk, annoyed. He'd trusted Carmen not to discuss this with their brother until they could meet face to face.

'Exactly as I said,' Alejandro responded evenly. 'I'm trying to get him to see that surgery is his only real choice. Carmen shouldn't have said anything to you.'

'Why not?' Sebastián snapped. 'I told you that I want to be kept informed.'

'You are.'

'Well, it doesn't feel like it from this end. I'm flying home—you can take over the talks here.'

'Why?' Alejandro demanded. 'I've told you…there is no real change.' He pressed his lips together rather than tell Sebastián he was overreacting. 'If there was anything serious I would have called you.'

'I just know that I need to see him,' Sebastián said. 'I can't sleep.'

'What time is it there?'

'Three in the morning.'

Alejandro took a breath, surprised at his brother's sudden sentimentality.

'All this talk of hospices,' Sebastián said. 'It wasn't even on the agenda when I left—'

'Sebastián, listen,' Alejandro cut in. 'It isn't on the agenda now…' He halted, realising that he was being selfish.

Usually he'd have hopped on a flight to New York without a second thought. But he and Emily were down to mere days, and Alejandro wanted all of them. Then he thought of what Emily had said—about how she wished she'd had a brother or sister to lean on—and knew that perhaps it was time to be that person.

'Of course,' Alejandro said. 'I'll organise my flight now.'

'Thanks.'

Alejandro had always kept things incredibly professional at work. So much so that when he buzzed down and asked her to come up to his office, Emily truly thought it must be about the website.

She hadn't actually ever been in his office.

There had been no need.

The Romeros really did keep themselves private, even if they both worked and lived on the premises.

His office was on the top floor, and it was quite a climb to get there.

'Wow!' Emily said, looking more at the gorgeous view than at the office itself. It was a bright blue morning in Jerez, and it was on full display up here. 'Is this all yours?' she asked, casting her eyes around.

'It is. Sebastián has the south wing.'

'You've had your hair cut.' She smiled, looking at his closely cropped hair and itching to run her hand through it, but refraining.

'I have,' Alejandro said.

He decided to deal with business first—or perhaps he was just putting off telling her about New York?

'I just spoke with him about the shot and he's fine with you using that image of him. He asks that you don't use any pictures that have Isabel in them.'

'Of course…'

'How's it all going?'

'It's coming together. The translator's been brilliant, and the IT guys are just checking the links. It will be ready to go live on Friday.'

'Great.'

With business out of the way, he still could not quite bring himself to tell her, and decided instead to delay, just so he could see her smile.

He stood up from his desk and beckoned her to come over.

'We're at work,' she said.

'I'm not summoning you up here for sex,' he said, opening up the latches on the window.

She frowned as she walked towards it, but then she saw that there was a view of the church spire, almost on the same level.

'There have been arrivals…' He pointed to the nest.

'When?'

'I only noticed them this morning, but I'd say they're a few days old…'

'I can't see…'

'Wait until she moves.'

They stood watching, waiting for the stork to move, and his fresh citrussy fragrance was strong.

'Did you spill your cologne?' she teased.

'No—why?'

'Just…' She shrugged, and then stopped talking as finally there was movement in the nest. 'Oh, my…'

There were three not-so-tiny chicks that she could see, and as she counted them it was with a smile. She stood there, feeling privileged to watch.

'You have the best office view, Señor Romero. I'd get nothing at all done if I worked up here…'

Alejandro briefly closed his eyes. 'No, it is I who would get nothing done if you worked up here…' he said.

He was tempted to turn her to face him, to share a deep kiss, but knew he had to tell her the real reason he'd asked her to come up.

'Emily, Sebastián just called…' He knew she'd hear

the more serious edge to his voice. 'I have to go to New York.'

'When?'

'This morning. Now. He wants to see our father for himself. All these discussions about a hospice have un-settled him, so I'm going to take over the talks there.'

'I see.'

She nodded, and he told himself that this shouldn't come as a surprise. From the start she'd known that the brothers were often away.

'How long will you be gone?' she asked.

'I don't know,' he admitted. 'Emily…' He was rarely hesitant, but he wanted to ask her to stay on, knowing he had no real right to do so.

As they stood there, staring out of the window, Emily watched one of the adult storks leave the nest and soar and knew she somehow had to leave just as gracefully.

Leaving Jerez was never going to be easy—Emily had known that for some time. But leaving Alejandro was an entirely separate agony she'd refused to address. Somehow she'd convinced herself that she'd know how to deal with it when it happened…that it was a future problem that she shouldn't dwell on.

But now the future had unexpectedly arrived.

She took a deep breath and the heady scent of orange blossom wafted in on the breeze and filled her nostrils, tickling the back of her throat. Emily licked her lips, a little wave of dread washing over her at all she would soon leave behind.

No, not dread.

She felt nauseous.

Again!

It had happened a couple of times in recent days, Emily thought, running a worried hand over her chin and feeling a fresh crop of pimples… She'd blamed them on his scratchy jaw, or the water…or…

'I'll know more once I'm there.'

Alejandro carried on talking, and thankfully her back was still to him, so he wouldn't see the look of panic that flitted across her features.

It was that paella from the market making her nauseous, surely. Only it had been as fresh as the breeze, and she knew it.

Perhaps she was simply lovesick, Emily thought as she stood there, battling the wave of nausea and frantically trying to recall when her last period had been.

She was on the pill, for goodness' sake.

Only she had been a little lazy in the times she took it, given she was only on it for the convenience of regular periods rather than protection or pregnancy prevention.

Oh, God, she'd been the one to refuse a condom that first time. She'd been more careful since, but that first night…

He'd wanted to be careful…whereas she'd simply wanted *him*.

Please, please, may she not have made things complicated.

Breaking up didn't have to be complicated. Alejandro had said that from the very start.

'You don't have to rush off…' Alejandro said, and though her back was to him he watched her shoulders stiffen and the way she gripped the window ledge.

He assumed it was to do with the conversation taking place—that his hinting that she stay on a little longer fell outside the boundaries they had so carefully put in place.

'I mean, the website is close to completion, and it's good that offers are starting to come in for you, but you can surely have a break between...' He halted, because for a brief second he could almost hear his father arguing with his mother.

'You don't need to go on tour so quickly, surely?'

Or, *'I know it's a good offer, but it's not as if we need the money...'*

All the reasons his father had used on his mother to keep her from leaving, to try and hold her back...

Four weeks into a relationship, was he starting to do the same?

'As I said, I'll know more once I get to NYC...'

'Of course.'

'Are you okay?'

'I'm fine.'

'Only you seem distracted.'

'No.' She turned and faced him. 'I ought to get back to my office...the translator wants to go through some things again.'

He caught her wrist as she went to walk out. 'Don't I even get a farewell kiss?' he asked, looking into her suddenly guarded blue eyes and completely unable to read her.

'Of course.' She kissed him lightly, briefly. 'Have a safe flight.'

'Emily?'

'What?' she snapped. 'Do you want me on my knees under your desk, or pleading with you not to leave?'

She shook her head. 'I thought you didn't like drama and emotion.'

So had he.

'We always knew this was ending,' Emily said.

'We did.'

'So you don't get to demand tears when it does.'

He would never quite know her, Alejandro realised as he watched her stalk out. He hopped on international flights without a thought, he was used to leaving with little notice, he didn't want tears over open suitcases.

He'd had a gutful of that growing up.

But he hadn't expected that he'd feel shut down by the sudden removal of her smile. That the end of them would be so…

Well, by his own standards this ending was perfect.

Emily Jacobs had given him everything he wanted: four weeks of passion and an easy parting.

CHAPTER THIRTEEN

BY SECOND BREAKFAST he had left the bodega. And now his plane would be well and truly in the sky, Emily knew as she stood in a pharmacy.

While her Spanish had vastly improved, she'd still had to look up the words for a home pregnancy test, but she had been sensible enough to dig out her own phone from the depths of her bag.

Prueba de embarazo.

She bought the kit and stuffed it down in the bottom of her bag, and then carried on with her long working day, sitting with the translator and the IT guys until late into the night.

Finally, she headed back to her apartment, listening to the music coming from the *taberna* and looking at the couples who dined in the courtyard.

Emily hated going up the stairs and knowing that there wasn't a chance of him being there.

More than that she hated the way they'd parted—how horrible she'd been when in truth she'd been panicking and scared.

She was oddly calm now, as she stepped into the apartment.

Alejandro was right—the flamenco doll was a little bit creepy, and she seemed to stare at Emily as she crossed the room.

'You'll give Willow nightmares,' Emily said aloud, turning her around to face the wall and sitting on the couch.

Above all else, she was missing him. Wishing he was somehow here, to tell her to get on with it, to just get up off the couch and do what she had to and find out.

Even though she'd braced herself for it, the two pink strips on the indicator still came as a shock: *Positivia*.

So she used the second test and checked again, but of course the answer hadn't changed: *Positivia*.

Oh, why hadn't she been more careful?

Her heart felt as if it were racing.

Alejandro could not have made it any clearer that he wanted short term, and she'd gone into this hoping for nothing more than a holiday romance…

No. Emily had to be a little more honest.

She might have arrived in Spain hoping for a holiday romance, but she'd been kidding herself that she could achieve that with Alejandro.

Her feelings for him had exceeded anything she could have anticipated right from the very start.

God, she'd made such a mess of things.

She could imagine Mariana's scorn, or the rolling of his sister's eyes, and Sebastián… But it wasn't their reaction that daunted her.

It was Alejandro's.

Alejandro was usually brilliant at switching off all feelings. But he'd arrived in New York to unexpected snow and a dinner to host, when all he wanted to do was close his eyes and think.

There really wasn't time.

With six hours tagged unexpectedly onto his day, by the time he fell into bed all he knew was that it might be better to leave calling Emily to when his head was clearer, tomorrow.

It was no clearer, even after he called.

'Hey,' he said. 'How are things?'

'Fine,' Emily said, in a voice that told him someone else was present. 'I'm just doing some last-minute updates.'

He waited while she excused herself from whoever she was with and felt a pang of guilt for keeping things so discreet that she hadn't even acknowledged his name when she'd answered the phone call.

'Sorry about that,' Emily said. 'Carmen's here.'

'Carmen?'

'She brought in some photos,' Emily explained. 'I'm just going through her bio and things.'

'She's changed her tune,' Alejandro said.

'Yes,' Emily agreed. 'She's being really helpful. Although…'

'Although…?' Alejandro pushed, and wished she felt able to state the obvious—that it was a bit too close to the deadline for Carmen to dump work on Emily, or for her sudden involvement. 'Although…?' he repeated, more gently.

'I'm just busy,' Emily said, clearly refusing to bitch about his family, and he adored her for that. 'How's New York?'

'Cold,' he said, and looked at the snow swirling outside the window of his penthouse suite, wondering how at the age of thirty-one for the first time he felt homesick.

Her sick?

'Emily,' Alejandro said. 'I don't like how we ended things.'

'No…'

'We can do better than that, surely?'

She said nothing in response, but he thought he heard her swallow.

'What are we going to do?'

He asked her the question he had asked on the first morning they'd kissed. What were they to do with this attraction, this ache, this desire and perpetual want?

Did he ask to upend her life?

Or did he upend his?

It was a bewildering landscape and like nothing he knew.

Or possibly he had once known—but his parents were such a poor example that he didn't want to draw on them.

Yet, here he was, doing just that.

How do you ask someone you love to stay?

How do you let someone you love leave?

Then she gave her response. 'You said it didn't have to be complicated.'

'I didn't know you were a virgin then.' He smiled as she gave a strangled laugh. 'And you hadn't danced for me then, *señorita*.'

There was a stretch of silence, but it was the nicest silence he'd ever known. Not a word was required for them to go back and live that night again.

It was a shared silence, he in his luxurious hotel suite

and Emily, he guessed, outside the office thousands of miles away.

Then the silence was broken as Carmen called Emily by the wrong name.

'Emile!' Carmen said.

Emily, he wanted to say.

'Tell her to wait…'

But of course she wouldn't do that.

'I'd better go.'

'I'll call you tonight.'

'We're having a pre-launch party this evening,' Emily said.

'Since when?'

'Carmen suggested it and managed to get Sebastián to agree. It will be nice for the IT guys…they've been brilliant—' Her voice was cut off as he heard his sister's impatient tone again.

'Emile?'

He gritted his jaw.

'I really do have to go.'

'*Do* you?'

He said it too harshly, still unused to switching those turned-off emotions back on, but his question was a loaded one—and it was not just about ending the phone call.

Work was not enough to distract him.

And, in the city that never slept, when usually he'd be taking his guests to a smart private club, Alejandro found himself back in his suite.

Unable to sleep.

The website wasn't yet live, but he logged in and looked at it. Emily's work was incredible. And then he saw pictures coming in on Carmen's social media, of the pre-launch party on the rooftop, the church spire in the background, the sun setting the sky on fire, and he felt more homesick than he had ever thought he was capable of being.

No, it was *her* sick—because she was wearing that grey top she had worn the night they'd first met.

Emily was smiling for the camera, but he could tell she'd been crying. And he felt a little mean that this insight pleased him because he hoped her tears were for him.

In the small hours—way before sunrise—it dawned on him that in trying to protect her from the backlash if he and Mariana's family found out about them, he might well have damaged her.

God, he had never ached to speak with another person more in his life.

Alejandro really wasn't one for making emotional phone calls, but he managed to convince himself he had a good reason to call—after all the website was going live today, and it would look childish if he didn't call to congratulate her.

He couldn't get through.

So he called his long-suffering PA, but she couldn't get through to Emily either.

His suite was warm, but he felt a chill of foreboding as he recalled his own words.

'My family don't always play nice...'

Yet Carmen was being...nice.

And Sebastián too, agreeing to a sudden pre-launch party.

While celebrations were commonplace at the bodega, he didn't understand his brother signing off on it, or his sister suggesting it, when they were so worried about their father...

Alejandro called his brother. 'Hey,' he said, 'how's Padre?'

'Doing well.'

'Put him on.'

'He's asleep.'

'Or is that me?' Alejandro checked. 'Am I the one asleep at the wheel? You're not in Madrid, are you...?'

'Since when did I have to check in with you?' Sebastián responded, and hung up.

Alejandro knew then that his hunch was right—he should have protected Emily better.

His father would have told Carmen that he had declined to marry Mariana, and Carmen would have told Sebastián about Emily.

Sebastián had never really been worried about their father moving to a hospice—it had all been a ruse to get Alejandro away.

Carmen dropping in with photos and being nice to Emily...?

Sebastián, whose mind was always on business, suddenly desperate to get home...?

Alejandro had known that he needed to protect Emily. That if word got out about them it would not be received well.

He called Reception at the office and asked to speak to Emily Jacobs.

'I don't believe she's in this morning,' came the reply.

'Of course she's in!' Alejandro was trying to keep himself from shouting. 'Okay, can you put me through to the housekeeper's apartment.'

There was a long silence.

'I'm sorry.' The receptionist finally buzzed in. 'There's no one picking up.'

He thought of her half-packed suitcase and their unfinished conversations…

Emily had left Jerez.

Alejandro was certain.

But it didn't change how he felt.

Alejandro wanted her smile, and her voice, and the way they were sometimes silent but still together in peace.

He wanted to be there when her star soared.

He wanted her for the long-term.

With Emily he would readily commit to being faithful.

It was love…

Emily wore her chocolate-brown dress for the launch. She'd make an effort for her final day of work, even though she was exhausted.

Last night's pre-launch party had gone on for ever.

All she'd wanted to do was escape and call Alejandro, resume their conversation. But Carmen had confided in her about a recent break-up, and Emily simply hadn't known how to excuse herself.

She'd sat in the courtyard with her teary new friend, drinking hot chocolate until two a.m., before falling into bed and a dreamless sleep.

Now it was eight a.m. on Friday morning and Emily had found out that she loved Alejandro more than she was terrified of telling him about the baby. Because, as she crossed the courtyard, for a fleeting second her heart soared.

She honestly thought Alejandro had returned.

The charcoal-grey suit, the thick black hair…

But Alejandro had had his hair cut, she remembered, and even before he turned around, she'd quickly worked out that it was Sebastián.

'Emile.' He smiled and shook her hand. 'It's all up and running?'

'Yes.' She couldn't be bothered to correct him about her name.

'It's looking great.'

'Thank you.'

'Could we speak in my office?'

'Of course. Now?'

'No rush—although I do have a lot on. And if you can bring your laptop? I want to check a few things.'

'Sure.'

He was Romero sexy, but with a more savage look, and his air was far more formal that Alejandro's had ever been. If anything, he was aloof.

'In your own time,' he said.

She took from that that he meant now!

Of course he was four flights up too, and by the time Emily got there he was sitting at a large desk on his computer, looking at the new website.

'The website looks excellent,' he said. 'I admit, I was cautious about commissioning an outsider, but I have to say it's worked well. As well as that, you came in on time…'

'Thank you, but there's just a few tweaks. I want to go up to the vineyard and get some images now that there are fruits on the vines.'

'There's no need for that. It's all just updates and minor things from here, and IT can sort all that out.'

'Of course.'

She chewed her lip. Was that it? She felt a slight flutter of panic as it dawned on her that this was officially her last day. Sebastián was here to wrap things up, thanking her for her work.

'I'm pleased I got back in time to thank you personally. My father is impressed too.'

'That's great,' Emily said, and then cast around to fill the silence. 'I was going to stay for the horse festival. It sounds so interesting...'

'Did you manage to get accommodation?' He sounded mildly surprised by her intention. 'It's usually booked out long in advance.'

'N-no,' Emily stammered, embarrassed. Her gorgeous apartment was clearly off the table.

Well, what had she expected? A holiday with free accommodation while she hung around waiting for Alejandro to return?

'I might look into finding a B&B...'

'Well, good luck with that,' he said, clearly meaning that she'd need it. 'All our accommodation is booked a year in advance for this particular festival.'

He was clearly not about to step in as her private travel consultant.

This really was it.

Of course it was!

Her contract expired today.

She'd allowed herself a couple of weeks' holiday, so her flight out from Madrid wasn't booked for a couple more weeks. More to the point, had she not been involved with Alejandro then her luggage and equipment would already be packed.

'Again, we're thrilled with your work, and we will certainly be happy to recommend your business.' Sebastián gave a tight smile. 'Now, just a few minor details… You have a company computer and phone…?'

'I do.'

She had to hand in her phone and laptop right there and then. It was the normal thing to do, but it felt as if they were being removed by force.

Her services were no longer required.

She made her way to her apartment, to think, but was met there by a rather harried-looking maid.

'There you are!' she greeted Emily. 'The new guest is waiting to check in!'

She had fifteen minutes to pack up her equipment and all the things she'd accumulated in her time in Jerez.

Emily went to say goodbye to the IT guys, but they were all busy and barely looked up to say goodbye.

Her welcome hadn't exactly been a warm one, Emily reminded herself as she came out to the courtyard. It had been a driver and a brief note from Sophia, suggesting she dine in the *taberna*.

But then she'd met Alejandro and everything had changed.

He wasn't here now, though, and without him she felt like an unwelcome guest at the bodega—one who had outstayed her welcome.

Even walking into the *taberna* felt a little daunting. Guessing she had no access now to the Romero table, she waited to be seated and was shown to the same small table where she'd sat on her first night.

She ordered coffee and a *tocino de cielo*, and as she cracked the caramelised crust with her spoon a waitress came over and rather pointedly put the bill down on the table.

No more free meals for her!

It wasn't that she minded paying, more that she was cross with Sebastián—not just for removing her, but for all the minor details that would be left out on the website. She'd wanted to picture this dessert, and to write about the nuns…there was so much more she'd wanted to do.

Or was it simply that she couldn't bear that it was over between her and Alejandro?

She ordered a glass of salted grapefruit juice, but it made her feel a little sick, so she asked the waitress for some water.

The waitress actually rolled her eyes, and Emily knew she was dragging things out.

She simply didn't know how to leave.

The worst thing was that without the company phone she didn't have Alejandro's number and couldn't call him. With her laptop handed over too, all channels of communication were gone.

Aside from the pregnancy and all things complicated, Emily wanted to say goodbye properly, and of all the regrets she had there was a ridiculous one—that she hadn't run her fingers through his short hair on the morning they'd parted.

'Emily…'

She looked up at the husky sound of a woman's voice, and although they'd never met she recognised her immediately.

'Mariana.'

'Oh, you know who I am?' Mariana said, as if surprised to be recognised.

'Of course.' She gave a tight smile. 'I've spent the past six weeks going through the Romero family's photos.'

As well as that she recognised the dangling diamond

earrings she wore. But of course she didn't mention that as the rather ravishing Mariana took a seat.

She had glossy black hair cut in a jagged bob. Her eyes were a vivid green, and she oozed nothing but confidence.

'I saw the new website,' Mariana said. 'It's impressive.'

'Thank you.'

'I remember saying to Alejandro that an outsider might give a fresh perspective.'

'Did you, now?' Emily said, trying to keep the sarcastic edge from her voice. She did not do sarcasm well, but that wasn't quite the way Alejandro had relayed it—he hadn't sneered when he'd said 'outsider', nor had he made her feel unwelcome with his gaze.

'Of course we have to attract the tourists…' She looked at Emily. 'Have you enjoyed your time in Jerez?'

'Very much.'

'I hear Alejandro has been an excellent tour guide…' She laughed at Emily's clear discomfort. 'Now, don't go getting all flustered.'

'I'm not.'

'But you are!' Mariana gave a low laugh. 'Emily, I know what's been going on. We all do. And I know how charming he can be…' She gave Emily a sympathetic smile, as if she were some poor, deluded fool to think that Alejandro would actually care for her. 'Alejandro might wander, but he always returns. It's been the same for as long as I can remember—especially at the end of the summer, when the tourists are gone… Of course, that was when we were younger. Now he has more sophisticated tastes…' She looked down at Emily's attire. 'At least most of the time.'

'Are you always this charming?' Emily asked, surprised at her own sarcasm and unable to believe her own boldness.

But even at her pluckiest, Emily was no match for Mariana.

'Go home, Emily—it's getting a little awkward now.'

'Awkward?'

'Embarrassing,' Mariana corrected herself, and then added, 'For you. No one likes to see someone make a fool of themselves.'

Emily didn't blush—rather she paled. Was that what everyone thought of her?

Mariana confirmed that it was.

'Seeing your puppy dog eyes following him around… Alejandro, he found it cute at first. But now he would rather do his brother's work in New York than be here, the place where he loves…'

Emily thought back to their first drive. How he had said that love only complicated things…that breaking up shouldn't be hard to do.

Yet here she was, clinging on.

Well, no more.

Homeless and pregnant was an exaggeration, but as she dragged her case through the *plaza* it wasn't far from how she felt.

The wheels of her case clacked over the cobblestones and it sounded like women walking and doing *palmas*, so close to the sound she loved, and so she went to drop in and bid farewell to Eva.

But, looking up to the studio, she saw she was mid-class.

Everything was just carrying on.

She sat on the edge of the fountain, trying to work out what to do. Whether to stay and try and find accommodation, or just head back to England…

'Fight your corner, Emily…' Alejandro had said.

She didn't want to fight her corner, though. She didn't want to plead her case, or ask if it was true that he was avoiding her.

If it was true, and he *was* avoiding her, then how did she tell him she was having his baby?

She reached into her bag to pull out her phone and call for a taxi. Perhaps her head would clear by the time she got to Madrid…

No!

She was tired of living like a frightened mouse.

What she didn't want to live with was regret.

Emily already regretted the way they'd parted, and she knew that the passage of time would only make things worse.

She dragged her case back to the bodega, unsure whether she was being completely pathetic or dreadfully brave, just knowing it couldn't end like this.

She was halted by Security.

'I'm sorry. Access is for staff only.'

'I am staff,' Emily said—she had been contracted until five p.m.

But it would seem that when the Romeros closed ranks and wanted you gone, you were gone.

'If you could watch my luggage for me.'

'Señorita!'

The guard called her back, but she was already clipping her way across the courtyard and through to the main building. Instead of taking the stairs to Alejandro's office, she headed for Sebastián's.

'*Señorita.*'

There was another guard, and he'd been clearly warned to stop her, but although that would once have terrified her, it actually reassured her.

They wanted her gone! But the Alejandro she knew would not hide in New York hoping she'd leave. If they were over, he'd have told her so.

She knew that about him, at least.

'*Señorita!*' the guard shouted.

'I need to speak with Sebastián,' Emily said, her heels ringing out as she took the stairs, wondering if she was about to be tackled, terrified she might be risking the baby.

But then she heard Sebastián's voice.

'It's fine.' He stood calmly at the top of the stairs, peering down and making her feel more dishevelled and inconvenient than ever. 'Come up, Miss Jacobs.'

Emily did so—slowly. Not really knowing what to say or do once she got there…just knowing she wasn't ready to leave.

Knowing, more importantly, that Alejandro would never subject her to this.

Sebastián's office looked out across the *plaza*. It was incredibly imposing, with an iron staircase in the centre, which Emily knew led to the rooftop terrace where those romantic images of him had been taken.

The smiling man in those photos was not the one she faced now.

'What can I do for you?' he asked.

'I have some things I'd like to discuss with Alejandro.' She took a breath to steady her voice. 'Is it possible to have his contact number?'

'No.' He was blunt.

'Well, is it possible that you can contact him and give him mine?'

'I'm sure Sophia has all your details. I'll ask her to pass them on. But right now I believe she's a little busy giving birth.'

'Can you call him for me, please?'

'Emily.' He came around the desk. 'I'm sure if Alejandro wants to contact you, then he will.'

'Well, I am not leaving Jerez until I've spoken to him.' Her voice was starting to rise.

'You are making a fool of yourself.'

'No!' Emily retorted. '*You* are being incredibly rude!'

There were tears in her eyes, but not of embarrassment, more of frustration.

'Your brother has manners, and as well as that he has guts, and if he wanted me gone then he'd have said so himself. If you don't give me his number then I'll—'

She never got to finish.

'You bastard!'

It was Alejandro, crashing through the door. An Alejandro she almost didn't recognise, because he was angry and menacing as he sped across the room.

'All this crap about wanting to see our father for yourself...'

He was furious, and for a moment she thought he was going to land a punch on his older brother, but instead they stood, two angry bulls facing each other.

Alejandro was no longer the reasonable one!

'Emily, go and wait in my residence...'

Alejandro didn't turn and look at her—he was still staring his brother down.

'Assuming my brother didn't change the code to that too. Go!' he said, still facing Sebastián.

Only when her footsteps had faded did he speak again.

'What the hell are you doing?'

'Taking care of business,' Sebastián said. 'You know our father's wishes.'

'He also wishes that his wife would come back to him. He wishes his cancer was gone without him having to make a decision about surgery. I am not marrying Mariana just because it suits his business plan!'

'It's been arranged since for ever.'

'It's been arranged since before I could talk,' Alejandro said. 'You all just assume that I'll marry her… that I'll stay because I was born into it.'

'What are you talking about?'

'I'm not sure I even want to be here,' Alejandro said. 'I don't know that I want to spend the rest of my career fighting against you and Carmen as you erase our mother from the brand.'

'You're not going to quit—'

'I wouldn't have to. I could just go and pursue my own interests like Carmen does,' Alejandro said, and raised a warning finger to his brother. 'Don't you ever mess in my private life again.'

'I'm trying to stop you from making a stupid decision.'

'Oh, and marrying someone I don't love is a better one?'

'You think you *love* Emily?'

Alejandro chose not to answer or correct him.

He would not be telling Sebastián that he knew for certain that he loved her.

Someone else deserved to hear that first…

She was sitting on the sofa where they had first made love, but jumped up when Alejandro pushed the door open and walked in.

'Well done,' he said, 'for standing up to him.'

He smiled when he thought of the words he had over-heard as he'd raced up the stairs.

'I don't think many people would dare speak to him like that…especially in his own office…'

'I'm not scared of Sebastián,' Emily said—because she honestly wasn't.

She was more scared of Alejandro's reaction when she told him her news—when he found out that their holiday romance had turned into something rather more permanent.

'What did Sebastián say to get you to leave?' he asked.

'Not much. He just thanked me for my work and got me to return my computer and phone. I didn't even have time to write down your contact details…' She shot him a look. 'When your family close ranks they really do it in style.'

'They do.'

'Then I found a maid waiting to service my apart-ment for a new guest. And then I was told you were in New York, avoiding me.'

'Who said that?'

'I don't want to tell you…'

'You have to.'

'Mariana. I went over to the *taberna*, to work out what to do, and she came and took a seat at my table and told me a few home-truths.'

'Mariana truths, you mean.'

'Perhaps… She said that it was getting embarrassing, me following you around like a puppy. That you needed someone strong. That you were incapable of being faithful.'

'No.' He shook his head. 'I am always faithful. It is long-term commitment I am incapable of—or thought I was.'

He took a breath, and as they had been on the night they had met his lips were pale, his eyes more serious than she had ever known them.

'Emily…' He looked right into her eyes. 'I told Mariana we were over in December, and since then they've all been worried. Usually we get back together, but I was serious when I ended it this time. I didn't know what I wanted, but I did know that it wasn't a convenient marriage. I wasn't just hiding you to keep Mariana happy. I was trying to hide how happy you made me…'

Emily frowned.

'The second Carmen saw us together she must have known this was something different.'

'How?'

'I was always a miserable bastard. Not depressed, or anything, but I don't strut and play models, as Carmen saw me doing.'

Emily smiled at the memory, and could see how it had been then that everything had started to go wrong.

'She must have called Sebastián straight away,' Alejandro explained. 'That's why I was suddenly needed in NYC. It had nothing to do with him being worried about my father, and everything to do with keeping us apart.'

'Why?' she asked. 'What could that possibly achieve?'

'Nothing.' He shook his head. 'Of course Sebastián

thought that in a few days I'd be over you, because
that's how his mind works, but I would have come to
England, or...' He looked at her. 'Or you'd have gone
to our hotel in Seville.'

'I couldn't afford a night in that hotel—let alone to
stay there and wait things out.'

'Then I'd have called Sophia for your number. Nothing he could have done would have kept us apart.'

He sounded so sure—a little like she'd felt as she'd
brushed past Security and demanded an audience with
Sebastián.

It was her secret that might ruin things, though.

They were too new to this, surely?

Too fragile for such news so soon in their relationship.

But his mouth was on hers and, rather then tell him,
she sank into his kiss. Allowing his mouth to smother
the pain of the past few hours and his tongue to chase
away any doubts as to their future.

And even if she *was* avoiding the truth, at least she
got to feel his shorter hair beneath her fingers, and feel
the anger she had witnessed with his brother turn into
passion.

They were, for the most part, still dressed. It was
naked passion that pushed up her gorgeous dress and
unzipped him. Desperate, necessary sex. And he
moaned as if he needed it every bit as much as she.

He made her frantic, yet as he thrust into her he
made this moment the only one that mattered. And
Emily knew she was a liar, because she closed her eyes
as she was taken on the sofa, just allowing herself the
bliss of being made love to by Alejandro before she
told him.

'Alejandro!'

She wasn't trying to tell him her truth. She just said his name as she orgasmed with alarming haste, and then closed her eyes as he followed.

They were breathless.

Joined.

Sated.

The closest they had been.

And yet she averted her eyes as he stared down at her, unsure as to his reaction when she told him her news, not wanting this moment to change.

He kissed her, then slowly stood and tidied himself. And as Emily sat up she watched him walk over to the record player and select the album she had bought for him.

She didn't want him being romantic when she had something so important to tell him, and yet it wasn't her words that changed the moment… It was Alejandro who rocked her world.

'Marry me?'

'Marry you?' She started visibly, and hauled her mind from babies to weddings.

'Yes, will you marry me? Emily, I know you have your career, and I swear I won't be like my father and hold you back. I've told Sebastián that I'm willing to pull out of the company if he tries to mess with me again. We could start our own bodega with my share of the land…'

'Stop!' She had a sudden image of her and Alejandro in a little hacienda, surrounded by vines, but then she shook her head, because she would never keep him from his family.

'I can't stop,' Alejandro said. 'Because I cannot stop loving you. So, whatever it takes…'

'Alejandro, please…' She made herself say it. 'I'm pregnant.'

She looked to him for a reaction, but he gave none.

'I *am* on the pill, but I must have messed up the times, or not been careful enough. I only used it to be regular in my periods…'

'Shh,' he said. 'We were both there.'

'And I know you don't want children—'

'It's more that I've never considered it a possibility for me…' He looked at her. 'Is that why you came back? Is that what you wanted to discuss with me?'

'Yes.'

She saw the dart of doubt in his eyes, as if he thought the only reason she had fought to see him was because of the baby, and it dawned on her that the very experienced Alejandro was as new to love and babies as she herself was. Maybe it was time to simply tell the truth and share this journey together.

'No. I came back because I didn't think we were ready to end just yet.'

He stared back at her.

'I came back because I wanted to tell you to your face that I'm…' she took a breath '…I'm not ready to give up on us.' She admitted her truth, although she covered her eyes as she did it. 'I love you. I have since the night we met. I've been lying all along.'

He smiled, unseen, and looked at the shyest, yet somehow the bravest woman he knew, and could only guess how hard it must have been for her.

Not just facing Sebastián and Mariana, but finding

out she was pregnant in a foreign country, by a man who… Well, he wasn't exactly husband material. Or rather he hadn't been husband material until he'd lain there on a lonely New York City night wanting simply to come home.

'Thank you,' he said, removing her hand from her eyes. 'For not giving up on us.'

He was too used to a mother who had angrily packed her cases at the first sign of a row, who had put her art and her career first, before everything, as well as a father and brother who always put business first.

'I know it's all too soon…' she said.

'No.' He shook his head. 'It's quick, and yet I love the thought of having a baby with you.'

And then he smiled a slow smile and answered the question he hadn't before. 'Romero Jacobs.'

'Sorry?'

He told her how her baby—their baby—would be named. 'It will be called Baby Romero Jacobs.'

'Oh!' That brought tears to her eyes.

'Why does that make you cry?'

'My father was always upset that I was the last Jacobs.'

'Oh, no,' Alejandro said, and ran his hand over her plump stomach, where their tiny baby grew inside. 'There are going to be many more…'

'Stop!' Emily laughed. 'We haven't even had one!'

But her protests were deliciously muffled by his kiss and his nicest words yet.

'We've barely even started…'

EPILOGUE

'THERE ARE RUMOURS...'

Sebastián knew he would happily end this marriage before it had started, even as they stood in the vestry, waiting to take their places for the wedding.

'A lot of talk going around—'

'I don't address rumours,' Alejandro interrupted. 'And usually neither do you.'

'I'm your brother, and if you're feeling pressure to marry because Emily is pregnant then know that—'

'Save the speech for the party,' Alejandro cut in.

He knew his brother had every reason to be mistrusting, but his caution wasn't required, and Alejandro would tell him exactly that.

'Can't you just be happy for me?' He glared at his brother. 'If you can't paint on a smile, then Carmen can be my *padrino*...' He gave a mirthless laugh. 'Then again, she is as suspicious of love as you. Listen, within an hour I will marry the woman I love. If you can't see that then it is *your* issue—don't make it mine.'

He could understand his brother's wariness—and in truth, if it were the other way around, then Alejandro might have doubts of his own.

Alejandro looked over to his brother. 'Just try...'

'Very well.'

But Sebastián rarely conceded, and as they headed out of the vestry to the church he halted his younger brother.

'Alejandro, I want nothing but the best for you.'

'Today, that is exactly what I am getting.'

'Then I wish you well.'

'Thank you.'

Their mother was arriving. Late to the church, as she'd no doubt planned. For there was no such thing as a discreet entrance for Maria de Luca.

She wore a silver silk dress and a high *peineta*—a traditional Spanish comb with an intricate white veil.

'Dame pan y dime tonto...' Sebastián muttered, and Alejandro actually smiled at the old saying.

It translated as *Give me bread and call me a fool*, but the real meaning was *I don't care what you think as long as I get what I want.*

It fitted their mother perfectly.

Maria did not blush or appear in any way awkward as she glided down the aisle and kissed a very tense Carmen—then affectionately kissed their father and took her seat by his side.

He'd had surgery the very night Alejandro and Emily had gone to his hospital suite to inform him they were engaged.

'We all know how Maria loves to upstage a bride...' he'd told him, as he'd kissed the top of Emily's head. 'Not that she'll be able to on this occasion.' Then he'd looked right at his father. 'It is something to look forward to, yes?'

José had frowned. This was not what he had intended for his middle child, nor the future of the business, and he had begun telling Alejandro so when Maria had walked in on them.

'Leave them alone,' Maria had said. 'I have never seen my son so happy.'

'You've not exactly been around to do so,' Alejandro had pointed out, but he'd been pleased to have his mother's support, for once.

'How long till the wedding?' Maria had asked.

'Four weeks.'

'Is that long enough for you to recover from surgery?' Maria had said to José. 'Or will the happy couple have to drop by the hospice?'

'*Madre...*' Alejandro had warned.

But, used to his wife's rather dark humour, surprisingly José had laughed. A wedding! Now that *was* something to look forward to.

'You can tell them,' Emily had said then, and Alejandro had gone over and sat on the bed, grateful to be able give his father their news.

'This is to go no further,' he warned, 'but Emily and I are expecting a baby in November.'

He'd watched his father start to cry, and Maria, who was the least maternal person he knew, had embraced his future bride.

A wedding and a baby!

There really were a lot of reasons for José to try and live...

Emily's *dama de honor* was, of course, Anna.

Little Willow had been unable to fly, because of her ears, but Anna's parents had come around somewhat, at least where their granddaughter was concerned, and she was spending her first weekend with them.

She'd come online now, and squealed when she saw Emily in her wedding dress.

'It's so pretty!'

'Thank you.'

It was pretty, and feminine, and actually quite bold for Emily, in the softest shade of magnolia. There were shoestring shoulder straps, and the fitted bodice hugged her curves and then flared into a gorgeous lace skirt, which would be perfect for dancing the night away!

'The flowers in your hair are so cute,' Willow said, as Emily lowered her head so that her goddaughter could see the delicate orange blossom tied through her hair. And when she looked at the screen Willow complimented her on one more thing. 'You're smiling.'

'I am.'

Despite her nerves, Emily smiled more readily these days although nerves caught up with her now, as they waited to head out of the boutique hotel where she had readied herself for the big day.

It was the *dama de honor*'s job to ensure that the bride and groom did not set eyes on each other until the bride's arrival at the church, and Anna was taking it seriously.

'You have to be late…'

'He'll surely be there by now.'

'Perhaps, but I have to be certain…'

Finally, Sebastián called and said they were safely in the church.

'Gracias,' Anna said, and rolled her eyes at Sebastián's sparse tones. 'He makes it sound as if the hearse has arrived.'

'I don't think I'm a very popular choice,' Emily sighed.

'Do you care?' Anna asked.

'I do,' Emily admitted. 'This is going to be my home, after all. Still, I'm happier than I ever thought I could be, whether they like it or not.'

They walked together beneath the arched orange trees and down the lane to the square.

The storks were flying high above the Jerez church spire and she smiled when she saw them, and remembered standing gazing up at them with Alejandro.

She'd felt so raw that day, so unsure of the world, and yet that night he'd taken her to bed.

Today they'd declared their love.

In front of a rather cold congregation...

Inside the church every head turned, and for a second she wanted to turn and flee. Alejandro had a lot of exes—Sophia, Mariana and Eva, to name but a few—and it was all so nerve-racking that she felt like the most hated bride in Jerez.

Oh, turn around, Alejandro, she thought.

But then her soon-to-be mother-in-law caught her gaze. Well, how could she not? Maria de Luca was no fading beauty, and she looked Emily right in the eye and caught her by surprise, for she was making a slight motion of her hand, as Eva would—one that told Emily to lift her head high—and then she made another gesture that told her to smile.

And that was what Emily loved about flamenco.

It gave her the passion and confidence to express herself, or to hide herself and then appear brave.

It taught her to look someone in the eye and frown or smile, and to talk freely with her eyes. And that was how she faced her groom as he relented and turned.

Confident and smiling, she walked up the aisle. It wasn't that he made her so. More that she was ready now to *be* so… As if, that first night in Jerez, he had encouraged her true self to emerge with his dark eyes.

'I've waited for you for a very long time,' Alejandro said as she joined him.

'I'm only ten minutes late.'

'No…' He made things clearer. 'I didn't know it, but I feel as if I've been waiting for today my entire life.'

'And me,' Emily admitted, as his hands closed around her trembling ones.

She had longed for a family, been desperate to fit in, to be less shy…

Now, thanks to love, all her wishes had come true.

* * * * *

Couldn't get enough of
His Innocent for One Spanish Night?
Then don't miss the next instalment in the
Heirs to the Romero Empire duet,
coming soon!

And don't forget to explore these other stories by
Carol Marinelli!

The Italian's Forbidden Virgin
The Greek's Cinderella Deal
Forbidden to the Powerful Greek
The Sicilian's Defiant Maid
Innocent Until His Forbidden Touch

Available now!

#4097 A BABY TO MAKE HER HIS BRIDE
Four Weddings and a Baby
by Dani Collins

One night is all Jasper can offer Vienna. The people closest to him always get hurt. But when Jasper learns Vienna is carrying his baby, he must take things one step further to protect them both... with his diamond ring!

#4098 EXPECTING HER ENEMY'S HEIR
A Billion-Dollar Revenge
by Pippa Roscoe

Alessandro stole Amelia's birthright—and she intends to prove it! Even if that means working undercover at the Italian billionaire's company... But their off-limits attraction brings her revenge plan crashing down when she discovers that she's carrying Alessandro's baby!

#4099 THE ITALIAN'S INNOCENT CINDERELLA
by Cathy Williams

When shy Maude needs a last-minute plus-one, she strikes a deal with the one man she trusts—her boss! But claiming to date ultrarich Mateo drags Maude's name into the headlines... And now she must make convenient vows with the Italian!

#4100 VIRGIN'S NIGHT WITH THE GREEK
Heirs to a Greek Empire
by Lucy King

Artist Willow's latest high-society portrait is set to make her career. Until the subject's son, Leonidas, demands it never see the light of day! He's everything she isn't. Yet their negotiations can't halt her red-hot reaction to the Greek...

#4101 BOUND BY A SICILIAN SECRET
by Lela May Wight

Flora strayed from her carefully scripted life and lost herself in the kisses of a Sicilian stranger. Overwhelmed, she fled his bed and returned to her risk-free existence. Now Raffaele has found her, and together they discover the unimaginable—she's pregnant!

#4102 STOLEN FOR HIS DESERT THRONE
by Heidi Rice

After finding raw passion with innocent—and headstrong—Princess Kaliah, desert Prince Kamal feels honor-bound to offer marriage. But that's the last thing independent Liah wants! His solution? Stealing her away to his oasis to make her see reason!

#4103 THE HOUSEKEEPER AND THE BROODING BILLIONAIRE
by Annie West

Since his tragic loss, Alessio runs his empire from his secluded Italian *castello*. Until his new housekeeper, Charlotte, opens his eyes to the world he's been missing. But can he maintain his impenetrable emotional walls once their powerful chemistry is unleashed?

#4104 HIRED FOR HIS ROYAL REVENGE
Secrets of the Kalyva Crown
by Lorraine Hall

Al is hired to help Greek billionaire Lysias avenge his parents' murders...by posing as a long-lost royal *and* his fiancée! But when an unruly spark flares between them, she can't shake the feeling that she *belongs* by his side...

YOU CAN FIND MORE INFORMATION ON UPCOMING HARLEQUIN TITLES, FREE EXCERPTS AND MORE AT HARLEQUIN.COM.

HPCNMRB0323

HARLEQUIN
PLUS

Try the best multimedia subscription service for romance readers like you!

Read, Watch and Play.

Experience the easiest way to get the romance content you crave.

Start your **FREE TRIAL** at
<u>www.harlequinplus.com/freetrial</u>.